HER STORY

of

JESUS

Katie Sampias

CALLA PRESS
PUBLISHING

Praise for *Her Story of Jesus*

Her Story of Jesus is an invitation to enter into the lives of women who discovered the transformative power of God's love through encountering Jesus. It is also an invitation to reflect on our own journey of faith. Through the stories that Katie has so beautifully penned, we are gently encouraged to open our eyes and look at Jesus. We are invited to discover more of His deep, unshakeable love for us, or to let Jesus shine His love and light into areas we have not yet trusted Him with. I was moved. I was encouraged. I was inspired. Accept the invitation to read *Her Story of Jesus* and enjoy the journey of discovery!

—**Liz Parker**, author of *Immeasurably More* (100ofthose.com)

These engaging and thoughtful creative explorations provide resources for reflection and allow readers to enter the stories of women in the Gospels and beyond in new ways. Katie Sampias brings the past to life, and invites us into a fresh world of seeing.

—**Joan E. Taylor**, Professor Emerita of Christian Origins and Second Temple Judaism at King's College London and author of *Boy Jesus*

What a joy to read! In her unique voice, Katie brings to life what it means to fall in love with Jesus. By taking the viewpoint of the women in the Bible, she artfully brings first century Israel to life. She simultaneously contrasts their daily lives with our own while drawing our attention to the similarities that do matter: the human need for love, compassion, and mercy. Katie is a master at reminding us that the Jesus we love and worship is just as applicable to our lives today as He was two millennia ago and that we are invited to have a deep, rich relationship with Him that alters every facet of our lives.

—**Leah Chrest**, Christian Meditation teacher and author.
(www.thecontemplativechristian.com, YouTube.com/c/christianmeditation)

Katie Sampias does with the women of Scripture what Dallas Jenkins has done with the disciples in The Chosen. She brings them out of the parchment and off the stained glass in ways both tangible and practical, fantastical but believable. And in doing so, she connects us to Christ with fresh curiosity that will send us back and back again to His Word. She shows us that we, too, have our own stories of Jesus as seen through these women. Real women. Just like us.

—**Melody Trowell**, author of *The Girl Whose Frown Shook the Ground*

Her Story of Jesus engages the reader's imagination in prayer and makes the Gospels stories come alive! Through Katie's story-telling Jesus becomes more human and real. The book will support both your personal prayer life as well as help you guide others in prayer with its mix of Ignatian contemplation examples and reflection questions for discussion and prayer at the end of the book. I highly recommend this book for anyone wanting to go deeper in their prayer life and get to know Jesus on a personal level.

—**Becky Eldredge**, award-winning author and spiritual director

Her Story of Jesus is not simply the stories of the women from scripture it portrays. It is, more importantly, the story of its author, of Katie Sampias's journey through hardship, kept and held by Jesus in the midst of uncertainty. This book is an example of how women can draw strength from the saints who have come before us as we abide in the persistent, unfailing love of Christ, able, like Mary, to rejoice in God our Savior.

—**Kori Morgan**, author of *Why I Dyed My Hair Purple and Other Unorthodox Stories* and founder of Inkling Creative Strategies

Her Story of Jesus by Katie Sampias is a true gem. The author transports us through space and time, right into a number of Gospel scenes, making us see, feel and smell Jesus through the eyes of different female Bible characters. This collection of short stories is a powerful blend of historical fiction, devotional, and a Bible study on another level. The readers can experience Jesus in a deep, emotional and imaginative way, thus enriching their spiritual life and drawing closer to God.

—**Hadassah Treu**, international award-winning writer at onthewaybg.com, speaker, poet, and author of *Draw Near: How Painful Experiences Become the Birthplace of Blessings*

Contents

Note From the Editor

Dear Reader,

At Calla Press Publishing, we are devoted to publishing true, noble, and lovely books that are both beautiful and biblically sound. Our mission is to spread the Gospel with every story we tell, and we have been blessed to partner with an amazing array of talented authors who share that vision and calling.

In *Her Story of Jesus*, Katie Sampias presents a unique portrait of Jesus Christ: a creative re-telling of the Gospel that introduces Jesus of Nazareth through the eyes of various women who encountered him throughout his lifetime.

Some of these women, like the virgin Mary and her cousin Elizabeth, are drawn straight from the pages of scripture. Their stories are familiar ones, having been told and re-told countless times in artwork, music, and film. Others, like Jarius' daughter (from *Talitha Koumi*—Jesus Heals a Little Girl") and Pilate's wife Claudia, may be less familiar. We know little about their lives apart from their cameo appearances in the Gospel narratives. Still others, such as Mara (from "Mara Serves at the Wedding at Cana") and Photini's daughter Sofi (inspired by "the woman at the well" in John 4), are not explicitly named in scripture, though they are inspired by real events.

Her Story of Jesus is a colorful tapestry of Gospel narrative, imaginative prayer, and extra-biblical research. As you engage with these stories, we encourage you to read the Gospel accounts from which they were drawn and to study for yourself the radical ways in which Jesus honored, esteemed, and ministered to the women of his day.

While portions of this book are fictitious, the heart of the narrative—God's tender compassion for women—remains true and steadfast. God loves women, and he graciously restores the dignity of those who have been downtrodden or cast out by their societies. We hope that with each story in this book, you will gain a fresh glimpse of God's gentleness, kindness, and love for all women.

Sincerely,
Allana Walker, Senior Editor

Introduction

I am delighted to be sharing with others my compilation of short stories I have written from the points of view of women mentioned, implied, or imagined in the Gospels. This work has been bubbling up within me for more than a decade.

Since I was a little girl, I have dreamed of publishing a book. For the longest time, I did not know what this book would be about, nor did I understand the process of writing it, but the desire was always there—even when I did not know how it would be realized.

Over time, I started to realize that writing was not something I could do alone. I needed to be guided by God. I thought more deeply about what he really wanted me to write and the stories he had buried deep within me. I found that writing this book was more about discovering what was already within me rather than creating something out of thin air. Many authors have said the same thing about their writing experience, but I did not understand what they meant until I experienced it myself.

I thought about what I was interested in, such as ancient cultures and, in particular, women's lives in those cultures. It became clear to me over time that I had the desire to write pieces based on the lives of women featured in the Gospels. These women witnessed something that not only changed them but also the world, and I wanted to experience their encounters with the person of Jesus—both his human and divine aspects. *Her Story of Jesus* is a work of historical fiction, which I have written by contemplating the Gospels, waiting to see what happens in my imagination, and researching where necessary. I have done this to expand and enrich my relationship with Jesus and to translate what happened in my imagination onto the page. I invite you also to engage with Jesus in this way by reading my stories, and perhaps through your own imaginative prayer. I hope that, as it has done for me, this will enrich your spiritual life and draw you closer to God.

I was about nine years old when I first engaged in imaginative prayer. I did not like my teacher, and, at times, I was scared to go to school. My mother suggested that I use imaginative prayer to picture where Jesus was in the room with me when I was afraid. I told my mother that I was sitting on his shoulders. My father used to carry me this way when I was a child, and I am certain that being blessed with a loving father was one of the reasons I had a clear, positive image of Jesus, which helped to calm my nerves during that year.

Somewhere along the way, my image of Jesus became fainter. Perhaps this had to do with negative experiences I had with men in my life or life's complexities and doubts I wrestled with as I grew older. I am not exactly sure why. However, later in my life, I was reintroduced to imaginative prayer through Ignatian contemplation.

The British Jesuits describe Ignatian contemplation in the following way:

> Imaginative contemplation is all about getting to know Jesus. It is a method of prayer in which you imagine yourself as present in a Gospel scene, stepping into the story and encountering Jesus there. It was St

> Ignatius' firm belief that God can speak to you just as clearly in your imagination as through your thoughts. This way of praying will help you to see more clearly, love more dearly, and follow more nearly the person of Jesus Christ.
>
> The idea that God can speak to people through their imagination can seem a bit strange. Isn't this just making things up in your head? On the contrary, the imagination is foremost a gift from God in the same way that a person's intellect or memory is a gift from God.[1]

When engaging in this type of prayer, I found I was not just interested in contemplating the Gospel stories. I was interested in their minutiae. I wanted to know what, in fact, happened to the characters in the Gospel stories—who they were, how their encounters changed them, and details about the time and place in which they occurred. I set about researching the answers to these questions alongside my imaginings. Perhaps you could call this process "investigative imaginative prayer."

I was more comfortable writing from the perspectives of lesser-known characters first. I think this is because they have limited interactions with Jesus, if any, recorded in the Gospels, which meant there was at first no pressure to explore intense encounters with Jesus in my imagination. This allowed me to slowly become more at ease with him.

The first female character's story I wrote was that of Pilate's wife. While Pilate's wife does not have a personal encounter with Jesus, she does have a profound experience in a dream, which I was fascinated to explore.

Slowly, I became more relaxed about getting closer to Jesus. God gently guided me to write from different

[1] "Imaginative Contemplation: Our Spirituality," *Jesuits in Britain*, accessed August 11, 2024, https://www.jesuit.org.uk/spirituality/imaginative-contemplation.

perspectives at different times. It was not just the investigative imaginative prayer that helped me get closer. Many things were happening in my life, including healing I was actively seeking out through psychological therapy, as well as spiritual accompaniment (engaging in conversations about life and prayer with a trained spiritual director who helps guide a person in their prayer life), that helped me with this. I was blessed with many people who loved me, and I learned about Jesus through their actions. I also had many transitions and experiences during this time, which enriched my understanding of the stories and enabled me to complete them.

The stories of the little girl who is healed by Jesus and the little girl who meets Jesus when he is left behind at twelve after the Passover are the stories I started imagining and embarking upon after writing "Pilate's Wife." I believe God was gently drawing me back to explore the perspectives of these young girls, taking me where I was comfortable seeing Jesus more clearly: in my childhood.

After these stories, I was invited to experience Jesus' death and resurrection. Completing "Joanna Experiences the Resurrection of Jesus" was a milestone in my imagining. The fact that I could look up and see the resurrected Jesus showed that I had received a great deal of healing.

The stories of the wedding at Cana were written during my discernment for marriage and completed after I was married. Anya, the bleeding woman who is healed by Jesus, and the midwife who assisted Mary during childbirth, were next. These women have life-transforming encounters with Jesus, but they were not a part of Jesus' inner circle. After experiencing their stories, I was ready to experience Jesus through those who were presumably some of his confidantes: Martha, Mary (Martha's sister) and Mary (Jesus' mother).

The final piece I wrote was, in fact, the last story chronologically. "Photini's Daughter, Sofi, Learns of Her Mother's Fate" imagines the life of the daughter of the Samaritan woman. At that stage, I had experienced Jesus' life, mission, death, and resurrection, and I was now invited to see what the lives of those who had encountered him were like several years after his ascension.

Writing this work has been an imaginative pilgrimage through which I feel I have formed a more intricate vision of Jesus in my mind and heart. Along the way, I have also become more comfortable with Jesus and found it easier to sense him in my imagination when engaging in imaginative prayer.

I hope that by reading, contemplating, and/or discussing this book, you can enjoy an immersive experience and receive a fresh take on the Gospels that enriches and nourishes your faith. Or, if you are someone who does not identify as a believer, I hope it increases your understanding of Jesus. Perhaps you may also like to engage in imaginative prayer of your own to see how the Gospels speak to you in this way. What you experience by inserting yourself into the Gospel stories may completely differ from what I have described in my stories. God speaks to each of us individually and uniquely. If I were to sit down and write these stories at a different time in my life, they could turn out very differently. However, no matter how we experience the Gospels, God meets us where we are, and that is what I understand as part of the mystery of their being the "living word." I think this is a beautiful thing.

The order of the stories in this book is chronological. They follow the trajectory of Jesus' life from his birth to his death and resurrection. The last two stories also imagine what life was like for women beyond his ascension.

At the end of the stories, I have included a suggested, optional format for group sharing.

Following this suggested format, I have included some reflections on my stories. The purpose of these reflections is to provide context, either historical or about my personal journey in writing these stories. It is also an invitation to dive deeper and to meditate on details you may not have noticed before in the Gospel stories. Lastly, I have included suggested questions that you may like to consider by yourself or with a small group or book club. My questions are only suggestions, so please feel free to contemplate or discuss anything that comes to mind.

Mary is Overshadowed by the Holy Spirit and Visits Elizabeth

Based on Luke 1:26–80

Mary knelt on a simple straw mat and focused her attention on the thick, brown linen garment she was cleaning over a wooden washboard. Some of her dark locks had escaped from her headpiece, and a few beads of sweat rested on her lightly lined forehead. She moved her small mouth from side to side as her mind contemplated solutions to her dilemma. Her cousin Elizabeth stood nearby, with her hands on her hips, leaning slightly backward, bracing her pregnant body. As Mary finished cleaning each outfit with lye and salt, Elizabeth took them and hobbled over to a small rack to hang them to dry.

While they focused on completing tasks that Elizabeth could not complete alone—cooking, making olive oil and wine, preparing crops for market, among other things—they proffered ideas about how to address the problems each of them was facing, but thus far, they had not made any satisfactory plans.

"Perhaps you can stay here until your baby is born, and we could pretend my child and yours are twins," Elizabeth offered.

Mary nodded to signal to Elizabeth that she was digesting this suggestion. The two continued their work in silence for a few moments while Mary thought.

Mary then shrugged and shook her head.

"They will be too far apart in age, Elizabeth—people will notice . . . Oh, Elizabeth, what am I going to do? I was so naive after the Holy Spirit came upon me that when I told Joseph, I thought he would simply believe me. I do not understand what God is doing with all this—it seems such a mess!"

The two stopped their work, inhaled in unison while looking at one another, and sighed.

"I wish all this was not so hard on you, Elizabeth. You're having to do so much while you're pregnant! I want to do more to help you," Mary said.

"Oh, it's alright, Mary," Elizabeth assured her, taking hold of a garment Mary had just finished wringing out and moving over to hang it up.

"You are such a comfort and help to me! More than you know," Elizabeth said earnestly, looking directly at Mary.

Mary smiled admiringly at Elizabeth, and the two continued their work while contemplating each other's respective situations.

Elizabeth then offered, "All we can do is keep praying for Zechariah and Joseph—that God will heal Zechariah's voice and that Joseph will come around to see that what you have told him is true. He, too, is being called by God to do something momentous."

Mary nodded in agreement.

"Tell me, Mary, what was it like when the Holy Spirit overshadowed you?" Elizabeth asked.

"Oh, Elizabeth, it was such a glorious experience. Let me see if I can describe it to you."

"I always knew I was different. God told me when I was a child, in many different ways, that he had great plans for me. I was curious about how I could be like Elijah or Moses, as I was a woman, and sometimes I doubted my mystical experiences, but I was willing to do whatever God asked of me," Mary started gently.

"The day Angel Gabriel appeared to me, I found myself wandering the foothills around my hometown of Nazareth. I always loved to explore the hills on the outskirts of town. My parents did not like me wandering so far from home, but I felt so close to God there, drenched in his love painted by the fertile green slopes, their specks of white rock, and the pure air. As I stood looking down at the buildings of my community, life seemed so simple and peaceful. The clusters of white rocks, molded into humble dwellings set against intermittent shrubbery, did not betray the stresses of everyday life for most people in the area—worries about the volatility of work, high taxes, and health.

I was thinking about what had taken place earlier that week. My mother and father had orchestrated the signing of my betrothal document to Joseph. I was happy about this arrangement, for Joseph was a good man. He was known in town for being prompt, punctual, and a gifted and fair tradesman. When Joseph looked at me, I always noticed the kindness of his eyes. You could tell by looking into them that he was not a man who thought only of himself, but who deeply cared for others; he was always willing to listen and lend his support in whatever way he could. I thanked God for providing such a solid husband for me, and prayed I could fulfill my vocation as a loving and nurturing wife.

As I prayed, I was distracted by a small iris that captured my attention, and I wanted to study its intricate beauty more closely. As I inhaled its subtle perfume, a warm heat filled my body. I felt a popping, fizzing sensation within me. I had felt these sensations before, and I knew they were from God, but this time they were much stronger. The air swirled around me, almost like it was tapping me and telling me to stand and look up. And so, I did.

The sun looked like it had quadrupled in size. My eyes adjusted to its increased strength, and as they did, I made out the silhouette of an extremely tall male being. He smelled of cinnamon spice and rose perfume. His muscular body, imposing wings, and golden metallic armor-like clothing were equally striking.

'I am the Archangel Gabriel. Greetings, you who are highly favored! The Lord is with you.'[1] His face gleamed as he spoke to me.

My body froze . . .

I leaned forward eagerly and wide-eyed, my heart pounding in my chest. I knew this was it! I was going to be told what it was that God wanted me to do.

'Do not be afraid, Mary; you have found favor with God. You will conceive and give birth to a son, and you are to call him Jesus. He will be great and will be called the Son of the Most High. The Lord God will give him the throne of his father David, and he will reign over Jacob's descendants forever; his kingdom will never end,'[2] Archangel Gabriel foretold.

I was speechless as my mind boggled. *God wanted me to birth the Messiah???*

'How will this be since I am a virgin?'[3] were the words that tumbled out of my mouth.

'The Holy Spirit will come on you, and the power of the Most High will overshadow you. So the holy one to be born will be called the Son of God. Even Elizabeth your relative

---

1 Adapted from Luke 1:28 NIV
2 Luke 1:26:30–33 NIV
3 Adapted from Luke 1:34 NIV

is going to have a child in her old age, and she who was said to be unable to conceive is in her sixth month. For no word from God will ever fail,'[4] Archangel Gabriel responded confidently.

Something about how Archangel Gabriel spoke partially settled my nerves. I bowed my head. I was willing to do whatever my God wanted from me. I was filled with peace as I gave my consent.

'I am the Lord's servant,' I answered. 'May your word to me be fulfilled.'[5]

Archangel Gabriel disappeared.

As I stood up, I saw that a clear sort of film material obscured my view of Nazareth, and I looked around me and saw this had completely enclosed me in a dome. It drew me to look at the center of it and a small, bright light appeared before me, more vibrant than anything I had seen before. As the light grew, so did the popping sensations within me— still pleasant despite their power.

The light was small at first, but it began to expand. I opened my hands, looked towards it, and said, 'Be it done to me as is your will.' I began to be raised off the ground to float in the middle of the bubble. The light then continued to grow to fill the sphere. Although I was overwhelmed by the enormity of what was happening and what I was being asked, at that moment, I was deeply peaceful and knew that this was the right path for me.

All the goodness, warmth, and power of the light began to transfer into my body. My body felt like it was on fire, but not in a painful way. The light was within me, and I could feel another was within me.

I was gently lowered to the ground and found myself kneeling again, looking at the flower that had captured my

---

4 Luke 1:35–37 NIV
5 Adapted from Luke 1:38 NIV

imagination before this mystical moment. I steadied myself and looked up. My eyes took a few minutes to adjust after seeing such bright lights. Once I did, I could see Nazareth gently beckoning me home. However, I knew I needed to stay to process what had just happened, so I lowered my back to the ground and looked up at the sky and the clouds floating above me while I thought about what to do next.

I knew I would have to tell Joseph, so I went to his workplace directly after this, filled with excitement.

The familiar sounds of thumping hammers and the tinkling of tools greeted me. Joseph put his tools down as I approached him.

I delightedly related my experience to Joseph, but I was unprepared for the reaction I received. My stomach tightened as I watched the color drain from his face. He looked so sad and disappointed in me. I could tell by his reaction that he believed me to have done the unthinkable and that I had made up some unbelievable story to cover for my transgression.

Joseph did not react angrily, but it was as if a huge weight had landed on his shoulders. It made him immediately look older, and I knew I needed to leave, so I despondently returned to my home. I was still filled with wonder despite Joseph's reaction, although it did make me doubt my experience. Was I hallucinating?

When I arrived home, my mother called for me to sit down and speak with her.

'Something amazing has happened, Mary. My sister Elizabeth has conceived a child. She sent word from Hebron that she is having some trouble managing her household affairs. This pregnancy in her older age is proving difficult, and she needs help with the daily tasks. She will also need help once the baby comes. Your father and I think it would be best if you go and stay with her for some time. She also says that Zechariah has contracted some illness which has made it impossible for him to speak; naturally, this is also causing some difficulties.'

You would think that after such a supernatural experience, I would not have been shocked by this news, but I was still amazed that you had conceived, Elizabeth, and I was so happy for you. The news of your conception reassured me that my experience had been real. I was still trying to process Joseph's reaction but was excited to go to you. It would be a perfect way to distance myself from what I thought might happen with Joseph. I did not want to be around when word got out that he had ended our betrothal.

My mother explained the travel plans to me: 'Your father has arranged for you to travel with a family going as far as Jerusalem starting tomorrow, so you must pack your belongings tonight. You will stay with these folks overnight in Jerusalem and meet another family from Hebron there who will travel with you for the remainder of the journey. We will explain the situation to Joseph and his family. Your wedding will not take place for a few more months anyway, and we have not yet started on arrangements. I am sure they will understand.'

So that's how it unfolded, Elizabeth. After Joseph did not believe me, I was too scared to tell my mother and father, so they do not know."

Elizabeth shook her head in amazement, moved towards Mary, and embraced her in gratitude for sharing her story.

"We must pray more," said Elizabeth.

Mary began to weep, releasing a flood of built-up emotions—including warm gratitude for Elizabeth's presence and support.

"We must pray for guidance and peace, and we must ask Zechariah to pray with us," agreed Mary through soft sobs.

Over the following weeks, Mary, Elizabeth, and Zechariah settled into a routine of praying alongside one another. At sunrise, sunset, high noon, and before going to sleep at night, the trio would stand beside one another, open their arms, and commit their lives and situations entirely to Yahweh. Although Zechariah could not speak, he still prayed in silence. Mary relayed her transcendental encounter to him, and although Zechariah could not respond in words, he understood and believed her. He communicated to them with gestures that he, too, had experienced an angelic encounter just before he became mute. All three of them opened their hearts to God throughout the day while they performed their daily chores. The rhythm of prayer served to calm Mary's mind. Elizabeth promised Mary that she could stay with them as long as she wanted and that she could even deliver her baby there in Hebron if she wanted to. Mary resolved to accept this reality if it was the only way to proceed. But they prayed for a miracle—that Joseph would come to believe.

Every day, Mary prayed the following prayer aloud:

"My soul glorifies the Lord, and my spirit rejoices in God my Savior, for he has been mindful of the humble state of his servant.

From now on all generations will call me blessed, for the Mighty One has done great things for me. Holy is his name. His mercy extends to those who fear him, from generation to generation. He has performed mighty deeds with his arm; he has scattered those who are proud in their inmost thoughts. He has brought down rulers from their thrones but has lifted up the humble. He has filled the hungry with good things but has sent the rich away empty. He has helped his servant Israel, remembering to be merciful to Abraham and his descendants forever, just as he promised our ancestors."[6]

When the day came to deliver Elizabeth's baby, Mary stayed by her side while Zechariah went to summon the midwife. Elizabeth's labor was long, but by the grace of God, she bore a healthy son, and although weary and torn, the birth had not broken her body beyond repair.

Those first few days after her son was born were intense and glorious.

News spread throughout the community that Elizabeth had given birth. Well-wishing neighbors came to welcome the new baby and to provide food and other comforts. Mary, the only person in the household who had not just given birth and could speak, was tasked with welcoming and providing hospitality to these guests. She was tired from her own pregnancy, but she was so happy for Elizabeth that she bore this discomfort gracefully.

Once Elizabeth recovered, she and Zechariah decided to have the naming ceremony at home. There was so much rejoicing in the community that Mary, much to her relief,

---

6 Luke 1:46–55 NIV

had very little to do to prepare for this; the community organized who would bring what food to share and appointed an appropriate mohel to attend.

The house was full and merry.

When it came time to name the child, the mohel asked Elizabeth what the child was to be called.

Elizabeth smiled before she spoke.

"He is to be called John," she said confidently.

Guests exchanged confused glances, and murmurs swept across the group of guests.

"But no one in your family has that name!" one of the guests protested. The guest then turned to look at Zechariah, who was gesturing for a writing tablet. Once one was handed to him, he wrote on it and held it up.

"His name is John," the tablet read.

Just then, God loosened Zechariah's tongue, and he began to praise and give thanks to God.

"Praise be to the Lord, the God of Israel," Zecharaiah exclaimed, *"because he has come to his people and redeemed them. He has raised up a horn of salvation for us in the house of his servant David (as he said through his holy prophets of long ago), salvation from our enemies and from the hand of all who hate us—to show mercy to our ancestors and to remember his holy covenant, the oath he swore to our father Abraham: to rescue us from the hand of our enemies, and to enable us to serve him without fear in holiness and righteousness before him all our days. And you, my child, will be called a prophet of the Most High; for you will go on before the Lord to prepare the way for him, to give his people the knowledge of salvation through the forgiveness of their sins, because of the tender mercy of our God, by which the rising sun will come to us from heaven to shine on those living in darkness and in the shadow of death, to guide our feet into the path of peace."* [7]

---

7 Luke 1:68–79 NIV

Those in attendance were amazed that Zechariah's voice had returned and at these words he spoke. They did not understand what they meant, but they discussed them amongst themselves and wondered who John would become.

Once all the guests had left, calmness fell over the house again. Baby John and Elizabeth slept while Mary and Zechariah rested. Suddenly, they heard a voice outside.

"Mary, Mary!"

Mary went out to see who was calling her. It was Joseph! His face was white, and his eyes bore dark circles underneath them. As Joseph spoke, his voice shook.

"I am so sorry, Mary. I did not believe you. But since you left, I have had many vivid dreams. An angel visited me in my sleep and told me all about the son in your womb. At first, I tried to dismiss these dreams, but they became so intense that I could not doubt them any longer. I knew then what you experienced was real, and I am sorry I did not believe you at first. God has called me to be this baby's earthly father. I am truly honored that he has asked this of me, but it scares me, too. I am worried about not being good enough, about letting God down. But I have been told in prayer that I simply need to ask for God's guidance. He knows I can't do this all alone."

Mary leapt forward to hug him, her heart full of relief and love.

"Joseph, I am terrified, too. I do not know what this means, but I am determined to follow our God, and I trust he will show us the way."

Just then, baby John let out a cry.

Zechariah came to the door and placed baby John into Joseph's arms.

"Come in, Joseph," Zechariah said eagerly. "You have a lot to reflect upon. God's favor is surely upon you, but we know you may feel overwhelmed. Come, have some food, and hold this little one. He shall calm your soul. We are so glad you have come. We were not certain what God would want us to do if you had not. We have been praying for you."

Joseph came in and sat down with baby John. Color slowly returned to his face.

He felt calmed by the presence of Mary, Elizabeth, and Zechariah, who understood his frame of mind.

Mary's Midwife Experiences the Birth of Jesus

Based on Matthew 1:18-2:18 and Luke 2:1-21

I remember that night.

"Ouch!" I had been mending some clothes and felt irritated after pricking myself. I put my needle and thread down. I was tired, which was a sign it was time to stop.

But I found it hard to be idle. I held my hands up to my face and studied them. They were worn and wrinkled, but they were not fragile. They were the hands of a hard worker—a midwife who had delivered hundreds of babies in her career.

I remembered a time when these hands did not carry so many creases. Back then, I was full of wonder and amazement at the miracles I experienced in every birth. Now, I was detached and apathetic.

It was not only in my work that I felt like this. Most days, I was just going through the mechanical process of living. I found it hard to be happy for someone celebrating a success or milestone or surprised by something unexpected. I even struggled to be saddened by the death or illness of someone I knew.

I am not sure when or why this apathy began. When I started working as a midwife, I experienced the pain and triumphs of childbirth along with those I was supporting. I often wept alongside the mother when she held her infant for the first time. I descended into feelings of darkness and despair for days or weeks after a birth that had not gone as planned, when a mother or baby had not made it, or when a child had been born unwell.

Some emotions still rose within me from time to time. One of those was anger—anger at Caesar. I thought of the poor pregnant women who were forced to travel for Caesar's census. There was no point in wishing Caesar would make exceptions for pregnant women. Such a man could not understand the complexities of these women's situations or the fact that such journeys could induce labor. I warned the midwives I had trained that birth rates would likely rise during the census, and I also ensured that they spread the word to other midwives in the area. There would be a lot of women going into labor earlier than expected.

In the weeks leading up to the census, I supervised the preparation of baskets full of essentials for these mothers—swaddling clothes, sheep fat, and undergarments. We found women who could assist by making and delivering meals and other essentials to recovering mothers. They would need nourishment in their time of confinement. They would be without the comforts of their home and their families. We also encouraged midwives who had not recently practiced to ensure their kits were in order and to refresh their skills by attending births with more active midwives.

It was nearly midnight when the wife of a local innkeeper, Anna, knocked loudly on my door. I had just fallen asleep on my sleeping mat.

"Quickly! You must come," Anna said. "There's a young woman named Mary giving birth in the stable behind our inn. We had no room for her and her husband."

"You will need to help me," I told Anna, struggling to wake up from my grogginess. "We will need hot and cold water throughout the evening, and I presume there will be none in the stables." I tried to snap myself awake.

Anna agreed. Together, we hurried through the village to the stable where Mary lay. My anger toward Caesar simmered deep within my gut, bubbling up into my throat. My joints gave way as I stumbled over loose rocks on the road. My last week had been so busy—one, sometimes two, births per night, and my aging body was struggling to function without sufficient sleep. But I picked myself back up and continued.

When we arrived, I found Mary had been laboring for some time. She told me the cramps had begun that afternoon as they entered Bethlehem. At first, Mary thought they were the false pains other mothers had warned her about. Only in that last hour had she realized she was in actual labor. Mary told me she was unsure about dates, but she had thought she had at least another few weeks until the baby was due. She and her husband Joseph had planned to be back in Nazareth by then.

Although Mary seemed to have the same sort of anxiety that most women have when giving birth for the first time, she also appeared to have a deep inner peace and acceptance of whatever could happen. This peace puzzled me, but it also relieved me.

I got to work trying to move Mary into a position that would make her feel more comfortable.

"Alright, Mary," I said as she shifted on the straw, "Just focus on your breathing now."

Mary nodded and followed my instructions as best as she could. Her labor progressed well.

Joseph, Mary's husband, sent Anna home to rest after asking her where he could source the water. He built a fire so he could boil the water, and throughout the night, he brought whatever I needed from the inn. I was impressed by his humility and desire to be helpful. I had witnessed so many men who seemed indifferent to the work their wives were performing in childbirth. Most men would have made themselves scarce while Mary labored through the night. Perhaps not all men were like Caesar, I thought.

The baby was born just before dawn. As soon as I delivered him, I handed him to Joseph while I attended to Mary. Joseph sat down by her side so she could see him. His little, black button eyes opened for a moment to see what life was about. His parents, although exhausted, cradled him with adoring love.

A shiver ran down my spine. Suddenly, I sensed that this family and I were not the only ones present. These other beings were not of Earth. Their presence lifted my heart and eyes. The room seemed to have expanded—this baby had opened the door to heaven, and these beings rejoiced for the birth that had opened it.

I turned my mind to what needed to be done next, as the atmosphere was so consuming. It would have been easy to let myself be entirely distracted by the strange sensations, but I needed to remain focused.

I attended to Mary and then took the child from his parents to perform the routine checks to ensure he was healthy. As I held the infant, ripples of heat flooded me, pulsating through my body. The waves seemed to emanate from this child's tiny body. Memories welled within me—fond memories from my childhood and my early years as a midwife. Emotions I had not felt for years permeated my heart. The love of this baby and his family had broken a dam within me; all the pent-up joy and sorrow of the dam rushed through me. I wept.

I wanted to hold him forever, but I knew I could not. He needed to be handed back to his mother so she could feed him. I did not want to leave the stable, but knew I needed rest if I was going to continue looking after Mary and her child over the next few days.

Just before I went to leave, I saw a small cluster of shepherds standing nervously outside the entrance of the stable. Their eyes were wide with amazement, and their mouths hung open as they stared at the newborn through the doorway. Mary gently beckoned them to come in.

"Angels appeared to us while we were tending our flock," they explained to Mary and Joseph. "They told us that we would find a baby here lying in a manger—a baby who would change the world!"

Over the next couple of days, I visited Mary, Joseph, and their newborn son as often as possible. The baby boy proved to be robust and a good feeder. Every time I entered the stables, the sensations that accompanied his birth enfolded me once more, nourishing my body and spirit.

On one occasion, three older men wearing expensive, foreign clothes. arrived and gave Mary and Joseph costly gifts for the child. Their story about how they had been led to visit was similar to the shepherds'. They reported that they had been led to the child by a great star—which, in their culture, predicted the birth of a great King.

I did not understand what was taking place in this stable. The sensations and unusual events kept making me want to return and stay with the new family as much as possible.

On the eighth day after the birth, Mary and Joseph named their baby Jesus and had him circumcised.

One night, as I held Jesus while the new parents slept, Joseph started to thrash around in his sleep.

"No!" I heard him shout out.

He sat up, startled, puffing, his brow full of sweat.

As he adjusted to being awake, his eyes moved over to me as I held Jesus.

"Are you alright?" I asked when his eyes met mine.

"Mary, Jesus, and I will need to leave!" he said as he seemed to regain full consciousness.

My immediate response to this statement was to worry about Mary. I was not sure Mary would be well enough to travel. But the urgency in Joseph's voice was so intense that I decided not to protest. After all that had happened, I knew better than to question Joseph's judgment. I started thinking about how I could prepare Mary so that she would be as comfortable as possible for the journey.

Joseph gently woke Mary and whispered in her ear. She calmly accepted whatever it was that he said to her and came over to thank me for everything I had done during her birth and recovery. She apologized for having to leave so abruptly.

"It's my pleasure, Mary. There's no problem with leaving. I just want to ensure you are as comfortable as possible," I reassured her.

While Joseph hurried to pack up his and his family's belongings, I handed Jesus back to Mary and created a cushion from some rags for use while sitting on the donkey. I told her to tell Joseph when she needed a break. Mary listened intently and nodded.

Joseph, being a practical man, was a fast worker, and it was not long before he had saddled the donkey and packed. He took some coins from a pouch he carried around his waist and gave me some for my services. He also gave me extra coins and instructed me to give these to the inn-keeper and his wife, Anna, for the lodging and care they had provided.

I rummaged through my midwifery kit to see if there was anything else I could give Mary, but I could not find anything practical. I did find a small Hand of Miriam ornament made of wood. I had kept this in my kit in the hope that Yahweh would protect all the children and mothers I assisted during birth. I decided to give this to Mary for protection on her journey.

I instinctively knew Joseph and Mary wanted their departure to be as quiet as possible, so I silently hugged Mary and handed her the ornament. I nodded at Joseph, kissed baby Jesus on the forehead, and watched them leave the stables. Mary carried Jesus, and Joseph led the donkey down the dusty street. They had only a tiny oil lamp attached to the donkey to guide their way.

Now they were gone, I realized my heart was racing. I tried to calm my anxiety about their plight by focusing on where I was in time and space. Joseph's countenance had disclosed that whatever they were facing was something evil and to be feared. I was not sure what would happen to them after they left.

Focusing my mind did help, but as I calmed, I became more aware of a weight within me, a tugging on my heart. I knew this family did not belong to me—they were not even from Bethlehem—but I would miss them as if they had been my own, and I did not want to return to the stunted version of myself I had been before I met them.

The tugging disorientated me, and I stood still, staring blankly while I regained my bearings. Despite it, I was grateful to realize my body and soul had not rebuilt the collapsed wall within me. My heart remained open. I sensed a presence in the room from the heavenly realm that this precious baby boy had opened. It moved to linger over me—similar to the way in which a mother hovers over her newborn in the middle of the night when she wakes to check on him or her. Some of the weight on my heart had been lifted, and my body softened with this gentle gesture. I then realized that my eyes were begging me to close them, and the best thing I could do at that moment was rest.

I found a place to lay my head in the hay and fell asleep.

Sepphora's Choice: The Bride at the Wedding at Cana Recalls Her Betrothal

Based on John 2:1–12

Sepphora was stunned when her father first mentioned that he had received a proposal for her hand in marriage. Although sixteen years old, she had not thought the time for marriage would come so soon.

Sepphora had been around men all her life—her father and brothers—but the intricacies of marriage remained a mystery. Sometimes, she had imagined herself as the heroine in an ancient land, called upon to marry a mysterious man who was dark and attractive but needed to be tamed. She had been intrigued by the story of Esther living in the palace of King Ahasuerus, who used her feminine charms and intelligence to save her Jewish people.

On one of her outings to the center of town, the man who was now requesting her hand had seen her. Her father had received the proposal while buying timber and said it would seem only practical to consider it. The man was the second eldest son of the family from whom he had purchased his wood. His name was Alexander.

"Alexander has not yet received his family's blessing," her father admitted. "They are of greater means than us, and there may be some objections. I have every reason to believe he is a man of honor, but I will make further inquiries about this."

Sepphora shuddered at this last statement. How would her father be able to find out for sure that this man would treat her kindly? What if this man turned out to be like the ones she had heard horror stories about at the temple; men who became violent and hurt their wives—physically, verbally, or emotionally?

"What do you have to say, Sepphora?" her father asked. "What are your thoughts?"

Her father's questions broke her dark reverie, and her body shivered involuntarily.

"Sorry, Father, this has surprised me," said Sepphora softly, as her eyes stared blankly ahead.

Her mother glanced at her husband with raised eyebrows and then turned back to Sepphora.

"Are you alright?" her mother asked, moving towards her to touch her daughter's shoulder.

"I think I need to get away for a while," Sepphora answered, raising her voice. "I need some time to think about this. Maybe I could visit Aunt Mary? I know she has been feeling lonely since Joseph passed away. And I know Jesus is there for her, but maybe she would be glad of my company, too."

Sepphora's mother looked at her husband. Her husband nodded in agreement.

"I think that's a wonderful idea," her mother said, tenderly squeezing Sepphora's shoulder. "It will give you some time and space to think."

Mary welcomed Sepphora with loving hospitality. She was extremely grateful to have someone to chat with. Sepphora easily fit into Mary's daily routine, helping her with her chores. As their conversation flowed, Sepphora found relief in telling Mary her anxieties about marriage. Mary listened intently and did not dismiss her concerns.

"Spend time in prayer and tell God how you feel about this prospect of marriage with Alexander," Mary advised. "Marriage is a way of life in which a couple seeks to love one another, and the children that are born as a result are a physical manifestation of God's love for us. You will never find a perfect person. Any marriage you enter into will have ups and downs, good days and bad days. Joseph and I certainly had our share of difficulties to navigate together. But what made our marriage work through it all was our commitment to helping each other be the best versions of ourselves for God, each other, and the world. We put God at the center of our marriage and prayed for our needs, relying upon God to find a way to meet them. Ask God for wisdom to know if Alexander is the person for you. Try to learn what you can about him. Your parents are reasonable and will respect your wishes if you do not feel this is right."

As Sepphora and Mary discussed these things, a door opened, and Jesus walked in. He was carrying a hammer in one hand and, at first glance, seemed deep in thought about something he had just been working on. But these thoughts appeared to dissolve as soon as Jesus looked at Sepphora and Mary's faces.

He smiled and let out a laugh. "Oh, so quiet as soon as I enter! Sorry to interrupt. I'm just here to get a bite to eat," he said, casually reaching for a bunch of grapes sitting on the table behind Mary and some flatbread left over from breakfast.

He raised an eyebrow and looked earnestly at his cousin. "Alexander's a great fellow, Sepphora. You have nothing to fear. I see him fairly regularly with my work. His family is one of my suppliers. I must go today to get more supplies. Would you like to come with me? You may not want to meet Alexander in person, but you can wait for me while I do business. You can keep me company and get an idea about where he comes from."

Sepphora's ears tingled, and her hands began to sweat. She could not refuse this opportunity to learn more about her potential husband.

Jesus was one man in Sepphora's life she had always felt comfortable around. She felt completely safe and at ease in his company, and he often seemed to be able to read her mind before she even spoke. Because of this, in some ways, she felt closer to Jesus, her cousin, than she did to her brothers James and John, and even to her father.

As they walked along, Jesus asked about her parents, Salome and Zebedee, and their health. He talked about how much he missed his father, Joseph, even though it had been over two years since his passing. He shared how he had been so incredibly busy with his business lately but had managed to save quite a bit of money for his mother. Sepphora liked how Jesus was so open with his feelings about his father and talked about his death. Others in her circle so often avoided such topics. Jesus also told her some quirky stories, which made Sepphora's heart dance and her whole body laugh. It didn't seem long until they reached an estate at the edge of the village of Cana.

When they arrived, they found a few people tending to crops and cattle. At one end of the estate was a grove with the largest pistachio trees Sepphora had ever seen.

"Wait here," Jesus said. Sepphora stayed with the wagon and watched from a distance as a man came out to greet Jesus. Jesus gestured toward the trees, and the two men began walking purposefully toward them. The second man seemed to be advising Jesus on which to cut. Sepphora realized he must be Alexander.

Alexander seemed quite severe and officious at first, but then Sepphora noticed Jesus was working to soften him, and before long, the two men were laughing and sharing a joke. When Alexander smiled, Sepphora noticed little crinkles around his eyes. When he threw his head back and laughed, Sepphora's heart warmed. If this man could share a joke with Jesus, at least she knew they could share a sense of humor, and perhaps spending time with him would not be so different from spending time with Jesus—maybe it would come naturally and easily. Sepphora sat down on the edge of the wagon and lay back. It would be some time before Jesus finished and was ready to return to Nazareth.

Sepphora returned to Bethsaida a few days later. Her father told her that Alexander's family had approved the marriage, and the couple would soon meet in person.

When Sepphora met Alexander, her body softened, her jaw loosened, and her eyes lifted. Alexander was more of a listener than a talker. She was surprised that she did not feel self-conscious when she spoke of her interests and hobbies, and their exchanges flowed freely with Alexander's adept listening skills.

Over the next few weeks, Sepphora met with Alexander and both of their families to discern if she wanted to accept his proposal. She discovered that she could laugh with Alexander just as freely as she laughed with Jesus. A new excitement about future possibilities started to enter her mind. She began to imagine the love she and her husband could nurture in her new family and the life they could create together. She imagined holding her children, sharing their happiness, and supporting them and her husband in difficult times. She experienced deep satisfaction when imagining these scenarios, but a heaviness also started to grow within her. She realized she was grieving for her childhood and the life she would be leaving behind.

Her days would be different, and the routines and rhythms she had known before would be gone. Her simple days of helping her mother run the household, balancing the books, and administering their family's fishing business would soon end. She had a busy life as a single young woman, but not so busy that she didn't have time to wander up and down the seashore. She would meditate on the different shapes and colors of the rocks and sand, lie on the shore, and watch the clouds roll above her as her brothers, father, and their men toiled on the water. Sepphora pondered how blessed she had been in her childhood. Her parents had nurtured her and provided for her so that she had never wanted for anything.

In addition to this sadness, Sepphora also experienced doubt. She began to wonder if Alexander was the best possible suitor for her. She started to worry that she would marry him only to find out later that there was a better match for her.

Sepphora struggled to reconcile these different thoughts and feelings so that she could make a clear decision. She did as Mary suggested and asked God to reveal whether the marriage with Alexander was right for her. As she listened for God's leading, she realized that any significant decision was bound to bring uncertainty and grief with it. Sepphora decided to base her decision on whether she believed this marriage to Alexander would best help her serve and love God and others, including herself.

Sepphora's family members had made nothing but positive comments about the prospective match. Her mother had noted that Alexander's practical bent would complement Sepphora's creative and imaginative tendencies. Her father had pointed out that Sepphora and Alexander shared a similar sense of humor, and when they were both joking together, their happiness was contagious.

Alexander's family had a good name, and Alexander lived up to his family's reputation in dealings with other people through his business and personal relationships. He seemed to love and serve God to the best of his ability, which included loving and serving the people in his life.

Despite the doubts and sadness still lingering in her mind, her heart was light and full when she thought about marrying Alexander. She decided to act on that and told Alexander she wished to accept his proposal.

Sepphora's attendants made the final adjustments to her finery. Once they were satisfied with their work, one lit a torch, and then the others followed, one by one, carefully and silently. The occasion was celebratory, but at this moment, the quiet also marked its solemnity. Sepphora stood tall as she prepared to approach her future..

Now it was time, she and her attendants began to move gracefully towards Alexander's home—the home that, after this evening, would also be her own. The air was warm and crisp, and a soft, amber light from the sunset glowed above the mountains on the horizon. The pebbles on the path crunched beneath her sandals, and her attendants began to sing.

Sepphora joined in their trills, letting her newfound peace swell within her. A smile glowed from within and filled her face as the group continued their journey to Cana, where Sepphora's new life would begin.

Mara Serves at the Wedding at Cana

Based on John 2:1–12

Mara changed into her nightclothes and brushed her long brown hair. It had been an exhausting day. Over the past few weeks, she had worked with the other household staff to prepare the wedding feast for her master and mistress's son, Alexander. She had worked many extra hours, but for the most part, she did not mind. The family for whom she worked had always treated her and her mother, Hannah, well, and she was happy for the bridegroom. However, the head steward, Josias, had been very strict about how to complete the preparations. Josias' volatility made her and the rest of the staff jittery.

Mara shuddered as a memory flashed in her mind. A few weeks before, she had taken a short break from her duties to visit her mother, who was working in the kitchen. Hannah had asked her to help by stirring a stew on the hearth while they talked, which Mara had diligently done until Josias unexpectedly appeared.

"What are you doing in the kitchen, Mara?" he boomed, his eyes flashing with anger and his face red and contorted with rage.

Mara, startled, had jumped, and the wooden bowl and its contents had smashed upon hitting the floor.

Josias' nostrils flared, and he moved forward towards Mara with his hands outstretched as if to grab her. Mara tried to move but found she could not. Her body had frozen.

"Josias!" Hannah shrieked, rushing forward.

Josais saw Hannah and caught himself. He lowered his hands. He did not apologize but darted out of the room without a word.

A shiver ran down Mara's spine as she recalled how precarious this encounter with Josias had been.

Josias had not always been like this. When Mara had joined the household staff as a girl, Josias was stern but kind. He had patiently shown those he was managing the correct way to do things. He often laughed and was cheerful.

However, his capacity to manage had diminished in recent years, which evidently frustrated him. Mara wondered if Josias' change in demeanor had to do with a back injury he had suffered several months earlier while lifting a large container. At times, she noticed that he looked like he was struggling to walk, and his face appeared strained with pain.

Hannah's health was also regressing, causing Mara to worry about how she would care for her once her mother could no longer continue working. She hoped the family who had been so kind to look after her as a child would also continue to look after her mother in her elderly state. If not, Mara would have to earn enough to support both herself and her mother and pay for a place for her mother to live.

As Mara lay on her sleeping mat, her mind drifted to the events of that evening. So far, the wedding festivities had gone well. The bride had arrived at the family estate beautifully dressed, accompanied by her bridesmaids. The arrival was a moving spectacle. Josias had been happy with how the first evening had gone. Light refreshments were served, and the families and a few guests who had come that evening went to bed with their stomachs and hearts full.

After the family and guests had retired, she, along with other servants, had laid the tables with decorations, cups, plates, and cutlery for the central feast that would occur the next day. Her mother and others who worked with her in the kitchen had prepared the food in advance as much as possible to reduce the work they would have to do the following morning.

The winemakers would deliver their wine to the local markets before dawn. Josias had tasked Mara with attending these at first light to purchase more. The servants had been purchasing wineskins over the last few months but still required a few dozen more to ensure there was enough to supply all the guests comfortably.

Mara thought over how she would carry out the following morning's task. She then closed her eyes, and exhaustion carried her off to sleep.

The sun was rising the following day as Mara walked towards the marketplace. Mara tried to focus on the present moment, putting one foot in front of the other while she pulled the carry wagon behind her, but a nagging fear gnawed at the back of her mind. What if something went wrong at the wedding feast tonight? What if something happened to upset Josias and threaten her and her mother's future?

Mara arrived at the marketplace. There were few customers at this hour, yet the tinkering sounds of workers arranging containers and pitching tents filled the air.

Mara proceeded toward the stall to purchase the wine. Barnabus the wine merchant was a short, stocky, hairy man with a jolly disposition. He sold goods—mainly fruit and produce—from a few different farms, but he also sold wines from the vineyards of the surrounding areas, all owned by the same local family.

"Good morning, Barnabas. I need to collect some more wineskins for the wedding festivities tonight. Josias has been counting heads and estimates we need about a dozen more. I will probably be making two trips to cart them back."

Barnabas rubbed his nose and leaned toward Mara with an apologetic air.

"I'm sorry, my dear, but there has been a family emergency at the vineyard for the last few days, which means I've had no wine delivered, and I have none to sell to you. The father has been on his deathbed, and I heard word he passed last night. I'm afraid all his sons have been with him and have been unable to deliver any goods to me."

Mara gulped. Her heart began to beat harder and faster. Visions of Josias' red-faced rants flashed in her mind.

Mara scrambled to think of possible solutions. She thought about other estates that could contribute to the wine supplies. But it was only a few hours until the official celebrations began, and she had other chores to complete before then. There would be little to no time to go and pick up wine from multiple locations. Besides, there was a chance that the wine might not run out. It was, after all, just as a precaution that she had gone to purchase more wine that morning.

Mara decided all she could do was return to the estate and complete her chores as quickly as possible so she would have time before the festivities to see if she could solve this problem.

When Mara returned, the estate was a hive of activity. Servants were rushing from room to room with flushed faces and tightened eyes. Mara knew her chores for the morning involved helping her mother in the kitchen, so she hurried toward that part of the estate. But before she could get there, she was intercepted by one of the other servants.

"Mara, we need you to help look after the children. Please come quickly. We don't have enough hands to supervise them while the servants dress their parents!"

Mara reluctantly followed and soon found herself running after three children, two of whom were toddlers, who seemed intent on ruining their beautiful clothes for the day's events. Her capacity to think about possible solutions to the wine issue was completely diminished. She was relieved when one of the other servants came out to tell her that she could return to her other duties.

She made haste . . . the main meal. As her eyes fell upon the jars of water and wine lined up along the courtyard wall, an idea sparked through her mind. She repositioned the water jars more prominently in the front and moved the wine further back. She then hurried toward the kitchen but was again intercepted by one of the other staff, who tasked her with ensuring that all guests were provided with enough food and drink before the formal ceremony began.

But even the ceremony did not bring any rest. Her presence, as well as that of many other household servants, was required in the kitchen. The dishes needed to be given the final touches in preparation for the main feast that would begin immediately after the official proceedings ended.

Following the ceremony, Mara began serving the dishes to the guests alongside the other servants. The guests seemed to have voracious appetites—either that, or there were many more guests than had been expected— for it was only a short time before they had consumed most of the main dishes. Finally, Mara had a moment of reprieve.

She slipped away to check how much wine remained. As she peered into the jars, her heart stood still. The supplies were almost gone!

Mara ran to the kitchen. It was no longer full of servants, but her mother was there diligently decorating a plate of char-grilled lamb with mint, coriander, and slices of pear.

"Mother!" Mara exclaimed.

Hannah looked up, startled.

"We have a problem with the wine. I tried to get more for our stockpile this morning, but Barnabas informed me that there was a family emergency at the vineyard, so there was nothing he could sell me today. I hoped we would have enough, but I just checked the supplies, and the guests have almost finished it all!

"I don't know what to do. Josias will be livid. I have been trying to direct the guests to drink more water, but my plan is not working, and we have more guests than I expected. I fear we will soon run out completely. Do you have some cooking wine in the kitchen that we could serve?"

Hannah put her hands on her temples and surveyed the room. Mara followed her mother's lead. But their search was soon interrupted as a middle-aged woman with alluring ocean-blue eyes stepped into the doorway of the kitchen.

"Forgive me for intruding. I am Mary, an aunt of the bride. My sister is feeling a bit under the weather, and I was wondering if you had some anise I could mix with hot water for her?" the woman asked in a gentle voice.

Mara and her mother, although distressed, immediately switched into serving mode.

"Yes, certainly, Mary," Hannah said warmly, swiftly moving across the room to where several small clay jars sat on a bench. She opened one that had been sealed with a cork lid and placed some anise seeds in a small cup. She removed a vat from the fire oven and used a ladle to pour some hot water from it into the cup, which she presented to Mary.

"Thank you so much! My sister will be so grateful. Forgive me, but I couldn't help but overhear what you said about the wine. If you excuse me for a moment, I will take this to my sister and then introduce my son, Jesus, who I believe will be able to help you."

Mara and Hannah exchanged looks of uncertainty, surprise, and embarrassment, but they looked back at Mary and nodded.

Once Mary returned, Mara and Hannah followed her outside. There must have been about three hundred people scattered throughout the courtyard in various groups. Some were sitting at tables set up for the occasion, while others were standing and chatting. The atmosphere was jubilant, but there was not yet any music or dancing.

Mara spotted Josias moving towards the corner where the drinks were arranged. Her stomach lurched. Josias was about to notice the problem.

Mara and Hannah followed Mary through the crowd to a group of men gathered under an archway leading into the courtyard. The men were having a lively conversation. As the women approached the group, Mara could see that one of the men was telling a story.

Dark curly hair framed his face. His eyes were bright and animated as he delivered his story. As he finished, the group burst into hysterical laughter. The storyteller noticed the trio arrive and, anticipating that Mary was going to ask something of him, grinned. "Woman, what does that have to do with me? My hour has not yet come,"[1] he asked. Mary met this comment with a stern look; intuitively, her son followed Mary away from the group so they could speak in private.

---

1 Adapted from John 2:4 NIV

Mara and Hannah were left standing near the group of men. An awkward silence hung in the air as they watched Jesus talk with Mary. Initially, he did not seem entirely convinced by what his mother was saying, but his eyes softened as he listened to her. Jesus took a deep breath and then nodded, agreeing to do whatever his mother had asked of him.

Mary returned to the group while Jesus thought for a few moments. Mary looked at Mara, Hannah, and Jesus' friends. "Do whatever he tells you!"[2] she said triumphantly.

Jesus returned and pointed to the edge of the courtyard, where the servants had placed six stone jars, the kind used for ceremonial washing, and said, "Come, let's fill the jars with water."

Water? Mara's heart sank. But she did not know what else could be done at this point. She and her mother obeyed Jesus' instructions by showing him and his friends where the well was. They soon filled the jars to the brim.

Mara anxiously surveyed the courtyard, looking for Josias. Had he noticed that the wine was almost gone? She could see he had, for he was walking straight toward her.

Mara froze.

"Here, Mara." Mara blinked. Jesus was trying to hand her a cup. She took the cup from him with trembling hands.

"Take this to the master of the banquet,"[3] Jesus instructed.

But before Mara could take the cup anywhere, Josias marched up to her with a strained gait. His face was red, and his nostrils flared as he bellowed, "Mara, where is the wine?!"

Mara did not know what else to do but hold the cup out to him, hoping that if he took a sip of water, he would stop shouting at her.

Josias took the cup from Mara and sipped. A puzzled expression fell over his face, and the redness faded. He stood

---

2 John 2:5 NIV

3 Adapted from John 2:8 NIV

up straight, and without another word, hastened away with a gait that showed no signs of strained mobility.

Mara fell to the ground, her body convulsing with uncontrollable weeping. Jesus crouched before her and patiently waited for her to look up. It took a few moments for Mara to realize that Jesus was there. As her eyes met his, her shaking body stilled, and she exhaled a soft sigh. Jesus remained crouched beside her, holding her gaze until she was calm.

Jesus held out a cup for Mara to drink. Mara took a sip. The water they had poured into the purification jars was no longer water, but wine!

Mara's whole body warmed as she drank more wine. All the hairs on her body stood on end, her skin glowed, and her face shone. She wondered who Jesus was, but despite this mystery, her heart and mind relaxed.

Music filled the courtyard, and it was not long before the guests began to dance. To Mara's surprise, some of the guests started asking her and the other servants to join them. Mara accepted their invitation, letting her confusion fall to the wayside as she savored the moment's sweetness. There would be plenty of time in the coming days to talk to the other servants about what had happened.

Mara saw Josias dancing with his hand around the bridegroom.

"Most people serve the best wine first and the lesser wine second, but you, Alexander, have saved the best wine until last!"[4] he exclaimed with a hearty laugh.

---

4 Adapted from John 2:10 NIV

Anya, the Bleeding Woman, is Healed

Based on Matthew 9:18–22, Mark 5:21–34, and Luke 8:40–48

Plop!

A water droplet fell on Anya's head. The moisture shocked her from her sleep, and she opened her eyes. Her sparse single-room dwelling was still dark, with just a hint of morning light creeping in through the small, high window overhead. A light rain pattered against the rooftop. Remembering the significance of the day, Anya felt grateful that the rain had awoken her despite her frustration about the dilapidated roof—a repair she had neither the financial means nor the physical ability to address. On any other day, the leak would have depressed her. But today, *today*, Anya hoped that her life would change, and that hope cheered her. She slowly rolled off her sleeping mat, carefully stood up, and moved to a small wooden chair and table where she sat down and peeled back a wrapping on some bread that her friend Sarah had brought when she had visited her the night before.

Sarah was a childhood friend. Although she was the same age as Anya, she looked like and exuded the spirit of someone years younger. Her hair was still dark and luscious, and her brown eyes sparkled when she spoke.

Sarah was naturally cheerful. Life had been kinder to her. Her husband was still alive, and her grown sons lived in the family home with their wives and children. Despite her good fortune, she was acutely aware of her blessings and sensitive to the plight of others, like her widowed friend Anya, whose children lived far away and who had endured constant bleeding for twelve years. She longed to find someone or something to heal her friend and had, like others who visited Anya to bring her sustenance and comfort her in her loneliness, told her stories of the new healer, Jesus. When Sarah spoke about Jesus, Anya could tell she was trying to restrain her excitement and was careful not to pressure Anya into seeking his healing touch. Sarah knew better than anyone else how many disappointments Anya had suffered from countless visits to healers and physicians to whom she had paid large sums—all to no avail. None of whom had been able to heal her.

"Word is that he has just been in the region of the Gerasenes, where he healed a demon-possessed man," Sarah had told her last night. "He is on his way back, crossing the Sea of Galilee with his disciples, and will likely be in this very town in the morning. There are reports that he and his followers will set up camp on the seashore."

Anya had tried to downplay her delight as she listened to Sarah's news about the healer. She was intrigued by these stories of Jesus. Despite all the disappointments she had suffered thus far in her pursuit of healing, the stories of Jesus had sustained her during the past few months. In her darkest moments, she would recall these stories, and they would give her hope. Something about the way people described Jesus made her feel optimistic about the possibility of being healed, and that optimism gave her peace about life in general. This peaceful hope did not make a lot of sense given all that she had been through, but based on everything her friends had told her about Jesus and his message about

God's love for the sick and downtrodden—not to mention all the miracles he had performed—Anya believed that if she could just get close to Jesus, things would be different. She *knew* he had the power to heal her because he carried God's love in his healing touch.

Anya had promised herself that if Jesus came to a place near her home, she would make every effort to get as near to him as she could. Anya thought it best if she remained as inconspicuous as possible so she would not need to discuss what she had done with anyone if Jesus did not heal her, and then no one could disapprove of her venturing out into public while still unclean.

After Anya finished eating, she bathed herself as best she could using a damp water cloth and balsam. She wanted to ensure the smell of her bleeding did not alert anyone to her presence.

Anya then slowly dressed in a plain cloak and covered her head with her shawl. The lackluster dress made her sallow skin look even more discolored. What would it be like to have the glow of good health in her countenance again?

The rain had stopped, and the clouds overhead were clearing as Anya left her tiny abode and headed slowly downhill through the village of small basalt dwellings toward the seashore. Although the dawn had broken, the sunlight had not yet infiltrated the cloud. There were not many people about at this time of day, and Anya was thankful she could travel to the healer while the village was quiet, as there was less chance anyone would see her.

When she reached the edge of the village, Anya hid in the shadow of the building closest to the shore, surveying the area to see if Jesus and his followers were there. Anya saw a small group of men and women around a campfire. Some were awake, sitting in silent contemplation. Perhaps they were praying, she thought. Others were still asleep, lying on the beach as the sun slowly rose further over the horizon. Anya crept forward and hid herself behind a cluster of plane trees not far from the group. Anya wondered which of the men was Jesus and debated how she should approach him. She saw that one man looked the most intensely engaged in prayer. That must be him!

Suddenly, Anya heard a man yelling to the group as he sprinted down to the beach. His face was red, and he gasped for air as he cried, "Rabbi! Rabbi! I need your help. My daughter is dying. Please, come to heal her!"

The commotion woke the followers of Jesus, and Anya's heart started to quicken. Anticipating that Jesus was going to leave with this man, she realized that it was now or never—she needed to muster up all her strength to get to Jesus as quickly as she could before he left.

Although it was only a few minutes before Anya reached the group, a crowd had formed around Jesus—not only his followers, but also other villagers who had heard about the rabbi's sick daughter and were curious to see what the healer would do. The swarm of people had started moving away from the campsite toward the next village.

Anya wove through the crowd with determination, desperate to reach Jesus.

"If only I could touch the hem of his garment, surely I would be healed," *she thought.* Then, with all her might, she stretched out her hand towards Jesus as she collapsed in exhaustion. Her hand just barely brushed Jesus' cloak as she fell to the ground.

Anya felt no pain as she lay on the damp, sandy shore. A strange warmth radiated through her body. Her skin began to tingle. All her hair stood on end.

---

1 Adapted from Mark 5:28 NIV

Anya was still lying on the ground, staring at the sandals of the people crowded around her, when she heard Jesus speak.

"Who touched my clothing?"[2]

Anya gulped. Her stomach clenched. Perhaps she had made a mistake. Had she miscalculated this situation? Before Anya could move, she felt a hand on her own and saw a man crouched before her, poised to lift her. The skin around his eyes crinkled as he smiled at her. Anya's heart skipped a beat, and her cheeks flushed.

It was as if, momentarily, she and Jesus were the only ones on the beach. All was silent. Time stood still. There was more gentleness in his eyes than she had ever perceived in another's. While her gaze remained transfixed on his face, his eyes replayed all the moments of her life to her. His eyes revealed an inner knowledge of her soul, her suffering, physical and emotional, and an infinite love for it. Anya's chest heaved, her jaw loosened, and the blood flowed through her veins with strong, steady heartbeats.

She let out a peaceful sigh as Jesus helped her stand. She was amazed at how nimble she felt as she rose to her feet. Could it be that Jesus had really healed her? Yes, she could feel it within her—her bleeding had stopped. The crinkles around Jesus' sparkling eyes deepened as he beamed at Anya.

Anya did not want Jesus to leave her, but she knew he must attend to the rabbi's daughter. Speechless, she could not find the voice to say, "Thank you," but her eyes conveyed the depths of her gratitude.

"Go in peace, daughter. Your faith has healed you. Be free of your suffering."[3]

----

2 Adapted from Mark 5:30 NIV
3 Adapted from Mark 5:34 NIV

With a parting smile, Jesus turned and pressed on with the rabbi. The crowd followed, leaving Anya alone to absorb what had just happened.

The sun was higher in the sky now, and the rain clouds had cleared to reveal a radiant day. Anya drifted toward the water. As she stood ankle-deep in the clear waves, she saw her reflection for the first time in years. Her skin was bright, and her nails and hair glistened with health. Anya waded further into the cool water, realizing that, for the first time in years, she could make concrete plans about what she wanted to do with her life. But there would be another time to make plans. Now, it was time for rejoicing, thanksgiving, and taking in the wonder of this glorious day. Anya ventured further into the water and lay on her back with her arms spread out like a star, gazing up at the clear blue sky.

Talitha Koumi—Jesus Heals a Little Girl

Based on Matthew 9:18–26, Mark 5:21–43, and Luke 8:40–56

It was only one day's journey back to our home. There were ten of us traveling together: my parents, a couple of my aunts and uncles, and their children—some younger and some older than myself. My mother chatted brightly with her sisters as they bounced along the path. The men also chatted, but their tone was more measured, so I assumed they were speaking about serious topics. Now and again, the adults would have to break their conversations to stop the younger children from venturing off the path to pursue a small animal, rock, or plant that had captured their interest.

The terrain was flat, and the road was well-worn and easy to follow, but a sickness hit me suddenly, attacking my insides. I felt the urge to vomit, but when my body convulsed involuntarily, nothing came up. The sun seemed to scorch me. My entire body felt excruciatingly hot. I lost my sense of balance, my body went numb, and my legs gave way. I collapsed onto the rocky path.

My family crowded around me. They shouted, panicked. My father crouched beside me. His brow furrowed and sweat glistened on his forehead. His face was red and distressed.

"My little daughter, are you okay?" he cried, as he reached for my hand.

I tried to speak, but no words came out. Before his hand met mine, everything went dark. The next thing I knew, I was lying in my bed at home.

I drifted between moments of consciousness and vivid dreams. At first, I dreamed about pleasant things, such as the wedding my family and I had just attended; I recalled the vibrancy of the ladies' robes and the excitement among the bride's attendants as they chatted, ate, and danced. I fantasized about my future wedding, imagining my wedding dress and the smiling face of my future husband.

As I bobbed in and out of consciousness, my thoughts and dreams became less pleasant. Sometimes, future potential suitors morphed into snakes and wild boars, and the incandescent dresses of the wedding guests became stained and worn. These dark dreams dominated as my body succumbed to its affliction.

Food and drink repulsed me.

I was only vaguely aware of the physicians drifting in and out of my room, prodding and examining me with strange instruments.

My periods of consciousness grew less regular. One time I awoke to the sight of my mother wiping my brow with a damp cloth. Her body convulsed as she wept, but I did not even have the energy to stretch out my hand to comfort her.

My body grew weaker and weaker. Sounds became muffled and muted, and my vision blurred until everything around me was vague and shadowy. My muscles grew as heavy as stones until I lost the strength to move them.

Soon, I grew too weak to think. My mind felt heavy, foggy . . .

Suddenly I was looking down at my body. I could hear sound, but it was muffled and muted. The air around me, if

I could call it that, was more like a film or liquid. The vividness of color was heightened.

An intense loneliness engulfed me, and a cold panic crept over me. I didn't know how to communicate or interact with anyone—to let them know how scared I was.

Was I still dreaming? Had I died? I did not want to die. I wanted to remain with my parents, I wanted to grow up, and I wanted to experience the wedding I had been dreaming about.

What if this is my eternity? I thought.

I did the only thing I could think of. I prayed.

A jolt of energy hit me. A blinding light had flooded the room. The walls seemed to pulsate from the radiance of the light. I could hear an intense buzzing that sounded like a giant swarm of bees.

I was no longer hovering, or dreaming. I was back in my body. A fresh warmth filled it, and I opened my eyes. I noticed that the source of the light was, in fact, a man. He leaned over me and took my hand in his. His grip was firm yet gentle. My hand tingled at his soft touch.

The warmth moved through the heaviness and clamminess of my body's sickness.

The bright light began to fade as the man's face came into focus. He looked intently into my eyes and smiled.

My whole body vibrated. My heart began to flutter, and then gradually it beat with a strong, steady rhythm. I felt I could run for miles and miles without fatigue, and light wanted to burst out from within me.

"*Talitha*, get up,"[1] he said calmly yet confidently.

The healing man pulled my arm to help me sit up, and then he turned toward my parents, who were standing in the doorway. I followed his gaze. My father's face was pale

---

1 Adapted from Mark 5:41 NIV

with shock. My mother had her arms around his waist, as if to keep him from falling over. The man who had healed me beckoned for my parents to come closer. My father slowly moved toward the bed with my mother's support. I stood up and rushed toward them, throwing my arms around their waists. My father gulped for air and trembled as he placed his hand on my head. Tears flowed down his face, and for a few minutes, he wept uncontrollably. A few silent tears ran down my mother's cheeks as she smiled at me. She rubbed my father's back to calm him, and his weeping subsided.

My father then released me, ran to my healer, knelt down, and kissed his feet.

"Thank you, thank you!" he choked.

That evening, my mother and father arranged a lavish feast to thank my healer, who, they later told me, was Jesus. My father stayed up with Jesus and his followers late into the night, discussing Scripture. My mother told me that I had been sick for over a month and had not woken for at least a week. They had heard that Jesus, known to have healed many people from grave illnesses, was in the area, so my father rushed to find him, and he came to heal me.

Several months later, My father, mother, and I walked to the outskirts of Jerusalem, where Jesus was rumored to be arriving for the Passover Festival.

A great crowd had gathered to see the now-famous teacher and rabbi. The air buzzed with excitement as Jews from all walks of life gathered outside Jerusalem in antici-pation of Jesus' arrival. The air reverberated with laughter and singing as we waited. Many people, including my father, mother, and I, had gathered some palm branches from trees along the road to welcome Jesus to the city.

I saw a figure in the distance, at the bottom of the rocky hill leading up to the city gate. He was riding on a donkey. My belly filled with excitement. As he came closer, the crowd became louder. They sang and chanted. I could see him clearly now—Jesus, the man who had healed me. Blood rushed through my veins, and my face flushed. This sensation made me feel as if we were all deeply connected, and as I looked around at those in the crowd, I could see they felt the same.

Jesus rode through the crowd. His face appeared serene, but as I looked more closely, I noticed that his skin was ghostly pale and there were dark rings under his eyes. As Jesus passed my family, he looked directly at me and smiled. He remembered me. I was flattered that Jesus knew who I was. His eyes were magnetic, just as when he healed me. As I returned his smile, I could see sorrow behind his kind eyes. I wondered why he looked so sad as he entered the city of Jerusalem. What could be troubling this healer who could raise people from the dead?

A Transformative Meeting
and a Last Act of Service

Based on Luke 2:41–52, Matthew 26:17–30, Mark 14:12–26, and Luke 22:7–20

I was so excited that he had chosen to hold his seder at our inn. I had spent the last few weeks ordering and planning for this meal. I wanted to ensure that Jesus, who had once made me feel so loved when I had felt so rejected, was served as well as he possibly could be.

On the day of the seder, I spent all day preparing the meal. I set the table with our highest quality plates and cutlery and added a few sprigs of ruscus and blackspot hornpoppies to ensure the room felt inviting.

His party started to arrive. They were a mixed bunch of unlikely companions. The group mingled and chatted freely despite their differences in background. I wondered how each had come to know Jesus, and I thought back on my first meeting with him.

The streets of Jerusalem hummed with activity. Carts waited on the dirt lanes outside the inns while men and women scurried back and forth, moving their belongings out of the inns and onto the wagons, ready for their journeys home. Children played in the dusty streets, and animals bleated as their owners saddled them up for the work they were about to do.

I loved the Passover festival—all the food, dancing, laughter, singing, and excitement of meeting new friends to play with. I looked outside longingly while I finished my chores.

There was only one thing I didn't love about Passover: It made me miss my old life and my papa. I had tried so hard to be a rock for my mother after my father abandoned us, but today, I could not hold back my emotions any longer. My mother heard my cries and came to comfort me.

"You know, child, you do not have to hold it all together for me. This is a difficult time for us both, but we will get through it together. We are so lucky to have each other, as well as my brother to support us here in his home in Jerusalem."

"I miss our old life . . ." I sniffled, "and I miss Father."

My mother held me close, and when my storm of sorrow subsided, she smiled at me and said, "Let's create something new together. I noticed there's some extra wood on the fireplace, and I know how much you like to make things."

For the next few hours, I focused on shaping my doll. I carved her limbs, head, and body and then crafted her clothes out of scraps of fabric that my mother gave me. She was small, and so, with my mother's help, I had been able to grace her with offcuts of gold and blue silk and some horsehair for her dark-brown locks.

I picked my doll up excitedly when my mother told me I could go and play with the other children who had just arrived in the city.

"Your uncle and I have everything under control," my mother said encouragingly.

I could not stop smiling as I approached a small group of girls and boys around my age and asked if I could join them. They seemed to be playing some kind of ball game that involved bouncing and catching within a court drawn in the dirt.

As I approached, the group stopped what they were doing and looked at me. I recognized one of them—the tallest and probably oldest of the group—a thicker-set boy who used to live in the same neighborhood as my mother and me. He smirked at me and lifted one eyebrow as he stepped forward, invading my personal space.

"Oh, look who we have here. It's the *bat zona*—daughter of a whore. Her mother left her father, and now she thinks she can still approach us to play."

The boy towered over me.

"What is this?"

He lurched forward and grabbed my doll.

"What a fine doll for one from such a filthy family."

With one sharp movement, he ripped off my doll's clothes, threw her to the ground, and rubbed her face in the dirt.

"There, that's where you belong—your doll, your mother, and you."

He cackled. All the other children laughed, too.

My eyes flooded with tears. I ran into an alleyway to escape their taunts. I tripped over a crack in the stone pavement and fell face-first, landing on my hands and knees. My tears made small mud puddles around me as I sobbed so hard I could barely breathe.

Within a few moments, I heard soft, tentative footsteps padding through the dirt toward me. I did not look up, as I was still too overwhelmed by my tears. The footsteps grew closer and when they reached me, a boy about twelve years old knelt and looked directly into my eyes. He had curly black hair, and his eyes were soft and kind.

"Hello, my name is Jesus. Do you mind if I sit with you?"

I managed to shake my head to let him know I did not mind.

Jesus carefully moved to sit down next to me and silently put his arm around my back. He did not say anything, and he did not leave me. With his comfort, my sobs subsided into whimpers and my tears stopped flowing. My chest began to draw more air in and out, in a slower and more even rhythm.

By the time I finally stopped crying, the noise in the streets had lessened. Jesus walked back with me to the inn. I asked him where his family was. He and I both looked around. The streets were almost bare. We realized his family must have left without noticing he was not with them. I invited him in, and my mother decided he must stay with us until we could locate his parents.

Jesus ended up staying with us for three days until his parents returned. Each day, he would go to the temple. Jesus liked listening to the rabbis teach and thought it would be easier for his family to find him there. He was an easy guest, so pleasant to be around. With Jesus, I felt more like myself than I ever had around anyone else. If I seemed downcast, he knew how to tell a joke or funny story to lighten the mood. And he helped with household chores in the inn wherever he could.

Finally, after three days, his parents returned. They found him listening to the teachers in the temple. Jesus brought his parents back to the inn to thank my mother and me for looking after him. They were warm and friendly people. They both seemed relieved to have found him and ashamed that they had left him behind. They stayed for a meal and one night at our inn before they set out again on their journey home to Nazareth.

Each year at the Passover festival, Jesus would come to see me and bring me a wood carving. The detail was impressive. He always captured the essence of the ones he was trying to bring to life so perfectly. Some of the characters had likable demeanors, while others looked like individuals who were not so easy to like.

During these visits, Jesus would tell me stories about the people he had encountered working in his father's carpentry business, and I would tell him about the exciting guests who had stayed at our family's inn. As Jesus and I grew older, our friendship grew with us. He took over his family business, and I married. Whenever he was in Jerusalem, he would come to visit my husband and me.

Once he left carpentry and started on his new mission, I saw less of him, but I followed all the reports about him. I heard about the illustrative and vivid stories he told and, of course, about the healings. When he was in Jerusalem, he would still take time to visit me, and sometimes, he would stay in my inn with his disciples.

This evening was different. When Jesus arrived, he did not have a wooden carving for me. He greeted me with the same love and tenderness that he usually would, but his eyes were heavy, and I could feel that he was deeply troubled. I remembered all the love he had shown me and the tenderness he had poured into the carvings he had gifted me. I willed myself to echo some of this back to him as I looked into his eyes and embraced him.

I knew he was in trouble with the authorities. There had been rumors about his entrance into Jerusalem a few days earlier and his anger toward the merchants in the temple. For every follower he accumulated, Jesus also had an enemy among the Jewish leaders. There had been conflicts surrounding him before, but I had never seen him *this* rattled.

I like to think my embrace had some effect on his nerves. He seemed to steady himself and began eating this meal with his companions. They all started to settle in and indulge in the food I had prepared for the occasion.

But then Jesus did something that made me realize something grave would happen to him.

He took some bread, broke it, and said, "This is my body, which will be given up for you."[1]

Then, in the same way, he took a cup after the meal, saying, "This cup is the new covenant in my blood, which is poured out for you."[2]

I did not comprehend what he meant by these acts, but I knew his life was in danger. I could not stand still after he left with his disciples. I began pacing anxiously. Beads of sweat lined my hands and forehead. I could not sleep at all that night. I was the one who answered the door early the next morning when one of his disciples brought the news that the authorities had arrested Jesus. My heart tore in two. I fell to the ground, weeping as I had over the destruction of my beloved doll, but this time Jesus was not there to comfort me.

"*I must try to see him,*" I thought. With this determination, I dried my tears and hurried out into the early morning to seek whatever news I could about Jesus' arrest.

---

1 Adapted from Luke 22:19 NIV
2 Luke 22:20 NIV

Pilate's Wife's Story

*Based on John 8:1–11; John 18:28-40; Matthew 27:11-26;
Luke 23:1-25*

Claudia's red and gold robe is torn. Kohl runs down her cheeks, mixed with tears. Two men drag her up the hill, through the dusty street, towards the Jewish temple. The two men are surrounded by about thirty others, all in austere religious garbs, a dress Claudia has only become accustomed to seeing after moving to Judea from Rome after her wedding. The men surrounding her smell of sweat, and they speak agitatedly to one another.

When they arrive at the temple, they push Claudia to sit on the ground at the entrance and send one of the group in to find who they are looking for. The messenger returns about ten minutes later, puffing, his eyes darting between the beady eyes of the others.

"He's not here . . . I searched through the whole temple, and he's not here," he reports.

"What do we do with the girl?" asks one of the men guarding Claudia.

"Follow the law . . . stone her," calls another in the pack.

Pontipor hurries to shut the window before the dust storm. She tries to do it on her tiptoes, careful not to wake her mistress Claudia. As Pontipor sticks her head out the window to pull in the pane, she notices a large group of people walking towards the main entrance gate, apparently unperturbed by the ominous weather. Some look like the Jewish religious men she sees when she runs errands for Claudia. Their hair is long and curled, and they wear stiff black hats on their heads. She notices one man in a simple white tunic being forcibly led by two men in uniform. She has seen him before.

Once she closes the window, she hears her mistress stir. When Pontipor turns to check on her, she sees Claudia sweating and writhing in her sleep. She walks over and squeezes her mistress' hand.

"Wake up, my lady . . . Everything is fine. You are safe here," she says softly.

Her mistress sits up suddenly. She opens her eyes wide and gasps. Her sweaty hair sticks to her forehead. She looks to her left and right. After a few moments of silence, she squeezes Pontipor's hand.

"Pontipor . . ." she says as she struggles to catch her breath. "Do you remember the time we were in the marketplace and we saw the Jewish priests dragging a woman through the streets? Do you remember how we followed them to see where they were taking her?"

"Yes, my lady. I remember they took her into the temple and asked a man there what they should do with her. He defended her, and she was freed."

"Pontipor, I had a dream that I was that woman, but there was no one to stop me from being condemned. The crowd was stoning me when I awoke," Claudia whispers in a trembling voice.

"My lady, that man is here. I saw a group walking towards the gate just now, and they are bringing him here."

Claudia flips off her sheets and bounds to the window, forces it open, and peers down into the forecourt. The air is reddening and becoming thicker with dust. She coughs. At the front of the group is Jesus of Nazareth, the man she and Pontipor had seen in the temple.

One of the men standing near Jesus at the front of the crowd raps on the large wooden door below. Claudia bites her lower lip as one of the servants answers. After a short conversation, the servant closes the door, and a few moments later, her husband appears at the entrance along with two of his guards, one on either side of him.

Pontius, as usual, has awoken early. He is already dressed in his Roman uniform. He wears a red sash over one shoulder to indicate his Roman authority, as well as an ornamental crown of golden leaves. His guards wear linen tunics dyed red, with leather breastplates to protect their chests.

"What do you want?" Pontius asks irritably.

"We have found this man subverting our nation. He opposes payment of taxes to Caesar and claims to be Messiah, a king,"[1] a spokesman for the group spits.

"If the case you find against this man concerns your own nation, go judge him according to your own law." Pontius sighs and turns back toward the entrance.

The spokesman moves forward towards Pontius. "Governor, we do not have the authority under our laws to put anyone to death, and this is the only punishment suitable for this man's crimes,"[2] he pleads.

Pontius turns back towards the spokesman and the crowd. Claudia sees that her husband's demeanor has changed. He

---

1 Luke 23:2 NIV
2 Adapted from John 18:31 NIV

looks around at the crowd in front of him. Claudia can tell that he is evaluating his options. She turns to Pontipor.

"Quick, help me dress . . . I must urge Pontius not to harm this man."

"As you wish, Madam," Pontipor acquiesces.

Pontipor helps Claudia put on a clean white robe and ties a golden tassel around her waist to define her figure. She pulls a brush through Claudia's hair as her mistress rushes to tie her sandals to her feet. There is no time for coloring her face. Claudia is fortunate. She has not lost any of her wholesome beauty and freshness since giving birth to her two sons, and she is not a lady who requires artificial color to be striking to the eye.

As soon as her sandals are secure, Claudia sprints from her bed-chamber, down the stone stairs to the foyer, and then out through the entrance to the forecourt. All eyes move from Jesus and Pontius to her. Pontius flashes her a questioning look.

Filled with a rush of confidence, she says, "Pontius, I must speak with you at once. It is urgent."

She moves closer and gently motions for him to enter the foyer so they may speak without being heard. He huffs, wipes his eyes, and follows her into the grand marble foyer.

"What is it, Claudia?" Pontius asks. "What could be of such importance that you must speak with me *right now*, when I am trying to keep the Jews from rioting?"

With tears in her eyes, Claudia clasps her hands together and pleads, "That man, Jesus, is innocent. You must not let any harm come to him. I have had a deeply disturbing dream about him this very night. Please do not harm him."[3]

There is silence as Claudia holds her husband's gaze, pleading with the warmth of her eyes. Pontius' shoulders

---

3 Adapted from Matthew 27:19 NIV

droop slightly, and for a moment Claudia sees *her* Pontius—the soft-hearted man who lives deep within her austere husband, masked behind his harsh exterior. She has glimpsed this gentle strength before in his tender glances towards the children and in his affectionate looks toward her. Claudia witnessed the power of pure compassion when Jesus rebuked the religious leaders that day at the temple—the day he defended that poor woman. Never had she seen a woman caught in such a predicament treated in such a loving, respectful way by a man. Claudia had never witnessed a man fearless enough to stand up to such a rabid crowd with no concern for how they would judge him. And now, for a moment, she sees a flicker of that same fearless compassion in her husband.

Pontius scratches his head and blinks. "I will speak with him further." He motions to his guards to bring Jesus in to speak with him.

As the guards lead Jesus into the foyer, Pontius clenches his fists. He does not look at Claudia. Claudia sees that Jesus' face is pale, with shadows beneath his eyes. Despite this, and his bound hands, he still stands tall. He shows no signs that the tension emanating from the crowd outside perturbs him. He stands silently. Pontius walks back and forth around Jesus with his finger on his lip. His gait is stiff and heavy.

"Are you the King of the Jews?"[4] Pilate says with both curiosity and mocking in his tone. Jesus replies, "My kingdom is not of this world. If it were, my servants would fight to prevent my arrest by the Jewish leaders. But now my kingdom is from another place."[5]

"You are a king, then!"[6] says Pilate.

---

4 John 18:33 NIV
5 John 18:36 NIV
6 John 18:37 NIV

Jesus says, "You say that I am king. But the reason I was born and came into this world is to testify to the truth. Everyone on the side of truth listens to me."[7]

There is a long pause. Pontius sniggers. "What is truth?"[8] he asks, shaking his head. Despite his sarcasm, his eyes eagerly seek an answer from Jesus.

Claudia holds her breath.

Jesus gives no reply.

Pontius huffs and leans forward impatiently. He raises his voice. "You know I have the power to have you killed?"[9]

Jesus does not react to this forceful tone but responds, "You would have no power if it were not given to you by my father in heaven . . . The one who handed me over to you is guilty of a greater sin."[10]

Pontius stands silently for a few moments, returning Jesus' gaze before looking away . . . With a smirk and a single chortle, another side of him surfaces, and he decisively turns and walks back out to the crowd.

The guards lead Jesus back through the entrance and outside, following Pontius. Claudia hugs the wall as she quietly drifts to a place where she can secure a view.

The crowd murmurs about the re-emergence of Pontius and Jesus. Claudia sees Pontius raise his right hand to signal to the crowd for silence.

He booms, "As you know, it is customary for me to release a prisoner for you on the Passover. Today, I give you two choices of prisoner: Barabbas, a convicted murderer and a menace to your society, or, Jesus, whose only crime is that he claims to be a king. These are your two choices."[11]

---

7 John 18:37 NIV
8 John 18:38 NIV
9 Adapted from John 19:10 NIV
10 Adapted from John 19:11 NIV
11 Adapted from John 18:39 NIV

Silence . . . and then a few disjointed cries.

"Barrabas! Barrabas!"

There is murmuring among the crowd, and then a small group of men starts shouting from the back: "Barrabas, Barrabas!"[12]

The shouting grows louder and louder until almost all the crowd joins in.

"And what would you have me do with this Jesus?" Pontius asks.

"Crucify him! Crucify him!"[13] the crowd screams.

Pontius walks towards a marble water basin a few meters from his chair.

He raises his arms, his palms facing the crowd, and cries, "I wash my hands of this man's blood!"[14]

He splashes his hands into the water of the water basin. As he removes them, he flicks the water off his hands and onto the crowd. He turns from the crowd and says quietly to one of his guards, "Have him crucified."[15]

Pontius does not look at Jesus as he walks back into the foyer. Claudia looks at Pontius with desperation, and although the pair's eyes meet, Pontius seems to stare right through his wife. He strides through the foyer and up the staircase that leads to his chambers.

Claudia turns back to look outside, watching as the crowd leaves the forecourt. They follow Jesus and those guarding him away. Visibility fades as the dust thickens. It is difficult for Claudia to see anything further than the length of the forecourt. She blinks her eyes, straining to see. The crowd is leaving, but she notices a slender figure still standing at the edge of the forecourt. As she peers through the

---

12 Adapted from John 18:40 NIV
13 Adapted from Matthew 27:21–26 NIV
14 Adapted from Matthew 27:24 NIV
15 Adapted from John 19:16 NIV

dust, she sees a woman peering back at her. Claudia meets this woman's eyes, she is struck by her resemblance to the woman from the marketplace—the one Jesus defended. The woman gives a short nod to Claudia, beckoning her, and Claudia, with a jolt, realizes it is indeed that woman.

Claudia hurries down the steps toward the woman. They follow at a safe distance behind the crowd.

Joanna Experiences the Resurrection of Jesus

Based on Matthew 28:1–20, Mark 16:1–8, and Luke 24:1–12

Joanna's mind wandered as she recalled the colorful events that she experienced in her privileged position as wife of Chuza, steward of the King.

She remembered sitting on a stone seat, looking toward a stage where two gifted singers caused her cheeks and ears to flush, sending chills of pleasure reverberating up and down her spine. The theater overlooked a luminescent red, burnt orange, and gold sky, which reflected on the waters of the Dead Sea below. Sitting on the horizon between the sea and sky were mauve hills. Throughout the amphitheater, gold, silver, and crystal jewelry dazzled in the setting sun as its warm rays reflected off the vibrant silk gowns and puffed chests of aristocracy surrounding her. A gentle wind tapped her face, and the glowing atmosphere caused her heart to flutter. She had thought it impossible to be happier than she was at that moment.

But that moment had taken place *before* her son had died. After her son had failed to wake at birth, darkness descended upon her, and an invisible silence engulfed her. Society continued humming, but she could not hear its melodies. The privileged splendor that surrounded her had lost all its color. She masked her grief by ensuring her appearance was immaculate. She spoke to no one, not even her husband, of her heartache.

Joanna's emotional distance had not gone unnoticed by her husband. Although their families had arranged their match, he genuinely loved his wife, and her unhappiness troubled him. Yet he did not know what he could do for her. He had tried to get her to talk about how she felt about her loss. But this only seemed to discourage her from communicating even more. The more he tried to reach out, the more excuses she appeared to have to spend time away from him. Chuza had reluctantly resigned himself to the fact that he could no longer connect with his wife.

One day, Joanna was surprised to learn that her soul was not cut off entirely from life. She discovered a movement that she could not ignore infecting the workers in Herod's court. The excitement led her to attend one of Jesus' gatherings.

At first, she watched from afar and attended purely out of curiosity to see the itinerant teacher who had become so talked about in Herod's household. But as she attended more and more gatherings, her interest grew. As she listened to his stories, her heavy cloak of grief lightened. She also watched at several gatherings as many sick people were brought before Jesus and healed.

Then, one day, when she had placed herself closer to the front of the crowd than she usually did, he approached her.

He walked purposely towards her, squinting with concern as he knelt on one knee before her. He looked directly into her eyes. Joanna was surprised that her body did not stiffen but rather softened under Jesus' gentle gaze. Jesus waited until Joanna had fully adjusted to his presence before he said, "It was not your fault, Joanna, and it doesn't mean God loves you any less than he does others."

Jesus' earnestness broke the marble casket encasing her heart. Her chest physically jolted from the shock, setting off fierce sobs. Her body shook with the intensity of her tears, and a deep pain within her was released. She had been too fearful to face this pain, to acknowledge that it had been preventing her from living.

Jesus touched her shoulder and waited until her weeping had subsided. He then smiled at her and nodded before rising to his feet and continuing to teach.

Since that moment, Joanna's life had changed. The darkness that had followed her for so long lifted, and light reentered. She found it not in glamorous events but rather in an increased awareness of nature's beauty, an appreciation for the love within others, and a sense of wonder at the simplicity of things like cool drinks on a hot summer's day and kind acts of strangers. These had all become vivid to her, filling her heart more than any fancy spectacle had in her past life.

But had her transformation been all built upon a lie? Jesus was dead! Dead! Was this new way of living also to die?

She looked around the room. The men mainly sat alone, in silence, withdrawn and sad. The women sat or stood in small groups, whispering and weeping. Martha was busying herself with practical matters—laying out food on tables in the center of the room so that all those present could eat when their bodies required it. There was an unspoken agreement that tomorrow's Sabbath meals would not be shared as usual.

Joanna looked over at Mary, Jesus' mother. Mary's skin looked deathly gray, a stark contrast to the usual brightness of her glistening skin. Mary's eyes were red, and she stared vacantly across the room, her body drooping with sorrow. John sat beside her with his arm around her. Both were silent. Joanna's heart felt crushed for Mary, another mother who had lost her son. She wondered what she could do for her.

Joanna realized she could do something that would assist, albeit in a small way. She could organize all the materials to ensure they could properly treat Jesus' body. There had not been enough time after his crucifixion to ensure this important ritual was carried out properly before his burial.

Planning the proper treatment of Jesus' body gave Joanna a sense of purpose, and having something to focus on gave her some relief from the awful thoughts and feelings that stormed her mind.

Joanna approached Martha and told her of her plan. She then left to return to Herod's palace in Jerusalem. It was quiet out in the streets, although Joanna noticed a few of Jesus' disciples had taken themselves outside to clear their heads.

Upon arrival at the palace, Joanna summoned her maid and asked her to prepare sandalwood, myrrh, and satchels to carry the precious elements. After receiving these from her maid, she returned to the disciples.

On the Sabbath evening, Joanna placed what she had gathered from the palace near a window in a smaller room adjacent to the communal room. This room faced east. Joanna, Martha, and the other women who planned to visit the tomb the next day slept close to one another near the window. They wanted to be sure the first light would wake them and that they would not wake up any men upon leaving.

Joanna rose first the next morning. She gently touched the other women one by one, and they awoke. In silence, they put on their headscarves, outer garments, and shoes. Though dawn had not yet broken, the cobblestones of the city street were turning a soft shade of blue as they started out to attend to their task.

The women's footsteps echoed off the walls of buildings they passed in the street until they exited the city through a stone-framed walkway. The sound of their steps softened as they transitioned from the cobblestone streets to the dirt road outside the city walls. Blue and gray were the dominant colors of the morning light.

The women walked in silence. Their sombre mood inhibited them from engaging in blythe chatter like they normally did when they journeyed alongside one another, accompanying Jesus on his ministry journeys.

The tombs were at the bottom of the hill of Calvary. The shrubbery was more abundant there as a small stream flowed at the base of the slope. As the women entered this area, the new day's light revealed an array of vibrant colors: shades of green leaves in the abundant shrubbery and a mixture of browns, blacks, and whites on the bark of the more mature trees. Pink and red splashes dotted the grass in the buds of wildflowers. The stream created a slight moistness that made their scent subtly perceptible even though only a few had barely opened.

The women barely noticed these changes in the landscape. Their thoughts turned to more practical matters as they neared the tomb.

"Who will roll away the stone from the entrance of the tomb for us?"[1] Martha asked.

Martha had barely finished her sentence when a sound like thunder engulfed them. The earth started shaking; the women lost their balance and fell to the ground. A tsunami of light burst forth from the tomb where Jesus' body lay, knocking the women to the ground and engulfing them with such vibrant radiance that they could not see. Two figures started to emerge through the brightness. They were human-like in appearance but taller and more ethereal than humans—angels.

---

1 Adapted from Mark 16:3 NIV

The pair looked at one another and then asked the women in unison, "Why do you look for the living among the dead? Jesus is not here. He has risen!"[2]

Joanna looked around to see to whom these figures spoke apart from herself, and to seek assurance that what she saw was real. But although she could see these two beings, she could see no one else as the white cloud had not subsided enough.

"Jesus is not in the tomb. He is risen!" The two figures continued.

With these words, the angels disappeared.

Joanna blinked and shook her head, wondering if she was dreaming, but then she became aware that she was lying on her stomach on the ground, her hands outstretched in front of her. The radiant white light was just starting to subside. She looked through the whiteness and could make out that what she was, in fact, holding onto were two ankles attached to human feet. Looking closer at these feet, she noticed two deep healed wounds in their centers. Joanna's body gave an involuntary shiver.

Although part of her wanted to look up, she resisted this urge momentarily. Her heart quickened, and her hands began to sweat. She was fearful that what she may see may overwhelm her. She knew she needed to look up. She took a deep breath and lifted her head.

Jesus' face shone like gold. Power surged within Joanna, and her body pulsated pleasantly from head to toe. Joanna's heart filled with relief and flooded with gratitude.

"There is so much more than you can ever imagine coming, Joanna," Jesus said, looking at her and smiling. He reached down and pulled her up.

---

2 Adapted from Matthew 28:5-6 NIV

Joanna embraced Jesus. Tears began to flow.[3]

____

3 Note that none of the Gospels specifically mention Joanna seeing Jesus in this way. All of the Gospels give slightly different accounts of the resurrection. Joanna is recorded in the Gospel of Luke as being one of the women who went to Jesus' tomb at dawn, witnessed the empty tomb and angels giving the news that Jesus has risen, but the Gospel of Luke does not specifically record her seeing the risen Jesus. Joanna is not mentioned in the other Gospel accounts of the resurrection. The Gospel of Matthew records that Mary of Magdela and "the other Mary" (possibly Mary of Bethany) went to the tomb and saw the risen Jesus in a similar manner to how I describe Joanna seeing Jesus in this story. I also had this personal experience in my imaginative prayer where I felt like I was laying at Jesus' feet for a long time and I was scared to look up to see his face. Looking up and being able to see Jesus' face was a big milestone in my spiritual pilgrimage writing this book.

Martha's Ministry in Antioch

Based on Acts 11:19–26, John 11:1–44, and Luke 10:38–42

The sun pinched at the exposed parts of Martha's skin. Martha had not slept all night. Her body was sore, her muscles tense. As she paced, she rubbed her neck, trying to alleviate her stress.

Martha paced across the pebbled mosaics of the courtyard, oblivious to the black and yellow orioles blossoming in the lush garden beds.

The mythical faces of the sculpted fountainheads eyed her silently as she muttered to herself, brow furrowed in distress, deaf to the playful gurgling of the water in the marble fountains.

Martha had arrived with Barnabas and a few others one week earlier to set up a base in Antioch, where they would continue to spread Jesus' message. The hunger for the Word was greater than they anticipated. Martha, Barnabas, and their friends had been inundated by curious Antioch residents.

Barnabas had indulged these visitors and spent hours conversing with them. But this method of evangelism was unsustainable. Martha told him things needed to be less haphazard, so she organized an event to take place that night. This would allow him to speak to a large crowd all at once instead of the steady trickle of people who came all throughout the day. She thought Barnabas had agreed to her plan, but in haste the previous evening, he and the rest of the group had gone to Tarsus to fetch Paul.

"How could he not realize that by leaving for Tarsus yesterday without warning, he has left me in a major predicament?" Martha thought. She exhaled exasperatedly. "Why does everyone think that whenever they feel inspired by God, they can simply go off and do these irresponsible things?" She asked this aloud to no one in particular, as no one was listening. She wrung her hands in frustration.

But then she caught herself. She knew she was doing what Jesus had told her not to do: worrying about many things. She shook her head and looked up to the sky, raising her hands with her palms open.

"Jesus, what would you have me do? I am here by myself, and a large crowd is coming to hear Barnabas tonight. I am your servant, and I place this in your hands."

Shortly after Martha prayed this prayer, a figure appeared at the entrance to the courtyard. She was a young woman, beautifully dressed in rich fabrics of gold and blue.

"My name is Calliope," the young girl said, speaking cautiously in Hebrew with an accent that showed her mother tongue was Greek.

"I am from Antioch and have just returned from Jerusalem. My husband and I went there for Sukkot and stayed on afterward for some business in town. I found the women carrying the message of Jesus and spent several days with them. Your sister, Mary, told me I could find you here and asked me to deliver this message. If you would like me to, I can read it for you."

"Yes, please do," said Martha, her eyebrows raised.

"My Dear Martha," Calliope began, narrowing her eyes as she focused on the page, "I write this letter to sustain you at this time in your mission. I know that when it comes to carrying on Jesus' ministry, once you set out in a certain direction you are sure God has called you to, there can be a period immediately afterwards when you doubt because nothing seems to be working. So, I am writing this letter to remind you of all we have achieved as a humble group of women in Jerusalem.

"We started very small in the days and weeks after we received the Holy Spirit. We witnessed many physical healings through Jesus' name. Women with ongoing ailments were restored to full health and sick babies were healed. Perhaps more importantly, many women became free to be more fully themselves.

"Our ministry grew slowly. Benefactors provided us with spaces, including homes where women fleeing violence and poverty could rest. There, they could also find fellowship with other women who wanted to become followers of Jesus.

"Our group became quite large and permeated the wider society. Perhaps this was not obvious to all observers, but I could feel the increase in peacefulness across Judea.

"But it was not without adversity or persecution. Sometimes, we did not know how God would provide for us, and he seemed to take a long time to answer our prayers.

"I pray for you in your new ministry, that you will receive guidance from the Holy Spirit in difficult times, and will not be disheartened when it is not clear how to proceed."

Martha's heart swelled. God had sent this message at the precise moment when she was tempted to despair.

"*Start small. Keep things simple,*" Martha thought. Her muscles relaxed and her heartbeat slowed. She remembered Jesus' words on another night when she had been worried about logistics.

"There is only one thing that matters, Martha," he had said to her.

Martha began to think about what that one thing was in this current situation. *The most important thing for people attending tonight is that they get to spend time with Jesus.*

Martha explained the dilemma to Calliope. "What do you think we should do?" she asked.

"Martha, the most interesting and wonderful thing for me would be to hear from you about your own experience of Jesus," Calliope said. Then she bit her lip and frowned, trying to think of solutions. "Could you speak to the audience?" she asked tentatively.

Martha tilted her head to one side as she contemplated this suggestion. She had never spoken in front of a large audience. She also could not speak Greek, which would be the mother tongue of most of the crowd, but Calliope could help with that.

"Do you think you could translate for me?" Martha asked, her eyes widening with excitement.

"Yes, I would love to," Calliope answered, nodding eagerly.

Small groups of people started to arrive early that evening. Although there was not much available to make them comfortable, Calliope and a small group of friends she had assembled at short notice greeted and ushered them in. There were families with young children. There were groups of men and groups of women who arrived together. Older women, some of them widows, came together, sometimes with a younger companion to help them. There was a range of skin tones among attendees, and Martha could hear various languages among them—Hebrew, Latin, Greek, and more.

Martha's chest fluttered and her heartbeat quickened. The demographics of the group were different from what she was used to in Judea. As she started to rub her hands together to calm herself, she was touched by an invisible presence. It was as if someone had taken her hand to steady it and help her stand tall. She was doing exactly what God wanted her to do at this moment—she knew it.

Calliope told Martha when the last guest had arrived. Martha drew her fists into balls and walked in front of the large crowd. Their murmurs subsided once they noticed she was standing in front of them. When there was complete silence, she began.

"Greetings, dear friends." Martha's voice faltered for a moment. She cleared her throat and tried again. "I am not the one you anticipated would be speaking today, and I am sorry about that."

Martha's voice cracked once more. She swallowed and then continued more evenly.

"My companion Barnabas was supposed to speak to you tonight. He is a gifted speaker, well educated in the Scriptures. Unfortunately, he and a few of our other companions were so overwhelmed by your enthusiasm to hear Jesus' message that they enthusiastically traveled to Tarsus to retrieve another great preacher of Jesus' word—Paul. Unfortunately, they have not yet returned. I am sorry that you cannot hear Paul and Barnabas tonight. I have prayed about what to do about tonight's gathering. In lieu of my companions' absence, I feel Jesus wants me to speak to you about my own experiences of him."

Martha paused and gripped her hands together. There were a few soft murmurs in the room. She waited until they settled, and then she continued with determination.

"I have two stories about Jesus that I want to share with you tonight. The first is about my brother Lazarus and how Jesus raised him from the dead. The second is about a conversation I had with Jesus that completely changed how I saw my place in society and my idea about how God sees me."

Martha paused for a moment. The crowd was silent; all eyes were focused on her.

"Jesus showed me that God is capable of much more than we could ever imagine even when we think all hope is gone. I used to live in Bethany with my brother Lazarus and my sister Mary. Lazarus was a stone mason. One time, his work became so demanding that he had to work relentlessly for months. He grew weak and fatigued, until he came down with some sort of illness that he could not seem to shake.

"He stopped eating and drinking until he grew so weak that he could not move. One morning, he did not wake. Mary and I did not know what else we could do, so we sent word to Jesus, asking if he could come and heal our brother. But, despite not being far away, he did not. Lazarus died. Mary and I were devastated. We anointed our dear brother with oils, wrapped him in burial clothes, and laid him in a tomb not very far from our home. Everyone in our village came to our house to bring us meals and pay their respects to our brother.

"I could not understand why Jesus had not come. I had seen him heal many other people with worse afflictions—people he did not know. And Lazarus was a good friend to him! Jesus had not been more than half a day's walk from Bethany. When I heard he had finally come to see us *after* my brother's death, I went out to confront him." Martha paused and then said, "I will try to role-play my conversation with Jesus."

Martha then moved her body so it was at an angle on one side of where she was speaking.

"Lord, if you had been here, my brother would not have died. But I know that even now, God will give you whatever you ask,"[1] Martha said, shaking her hands and looking wide-eyed at where she implied Jesus was.

Martha moved to Jesus' position and assumed a peaceful demeanor.

"Your brother will rise again,"[2] Martha said gently but firmly.

Martha moved back to her position.

"I know he will rise again in the resurrection on the last day,"[3] Martha said, her eyebrows furrowed.

Martha returned to Jesus' position and resumed a gentle, soft stance.

"I am the resurrection and the life. He who believes in me will live, even though he dies, and whoever lives and believes in me will never die. Do you believe this?"[4] Martha looked earnestly, pausing a moment before returning to her spot.

Martha's face softened and she said gingerly, "Yes, Lord, I believe you are the Messiah, the Son of God, who was to come into the world."[5]

Martha paused and turned to face the crowd.

"Jesus then called for Lazarus to come out from his tomb, and he did—burial clothes and all. All who were there could not believe their eyes."

Martha paused once again.

"Now, I see why he delayed his visit. He wanted to foreshadow his death and resurrection. He also wanted to show us—perhaps especially my sister and my brother—that even

---

1 John 11:21 NIV
2 John 11:23 NIV
3 John 11:24 NIV
4 John 11:25 NIV
5 John 11:27 NIV

when we think God has not heard our prayers, he has indeed heard them, and is still working things out.

"Sometimes, God brings things about in ways we never could have imagined—even when we are deep in death. That is how God works. He is always bringing dead things to life.

"God is always working. Today, all seemed dead to me, but I chose to trust God and to listen to what he was saying to me. I decided to speak tonight and lead this event despite Barnabas' absence."

Martha paused once again and surveyed the room. She was surprised that all the guests' eyes were still upon her.

"I need to share one more story with you tonight: the story of my interaction with Jesus when he was a guest at my house one evening.

"Jesus often came to visit the home that I shared with my brother Lazarus and my sister Mary. One day, I was working very hard preparing food and refreshments for all who were listening to him. I was the only one serving, and things got so busy that I became overwhelmed, angry, and frustrated. I felt the same way I did this morning when I started thinking about how all my companions had left me here in Antioch to orchestrate this evening by myself.

"My sister Mary was not helping. She sat directly in front of Jesus, listening to him. I was so exasperated because she was not thinking about the work that needed to be done—she was also the hostess! When Jesus paused his teaching for a time of refreshment, I took the opportunity to address this injustice.

"'Jesus, tell Mary to help me! I'm so overwhelmed, and I am the only one here to look after all of these people,'[6] I said to him exasperatedly, handing him a drink.

---

6 Adapted from Luke 10:40 NIV

"'Oh Martha,' Jesus said. He slowly sipped his drink and then smiled at me. 'You worry about many things,' he said, gesturing with his free hand to the tray I was carrying. 'Only one thing matters, and Mary has chosen this. That will not be taken away from her.'[7]

"This was definitely not the response I had anticipated from Jesus. I was taken aback and slightly irritated that he had not supported me—or had he? I needed clarification about what he meant and asked him to explain. He told me that my place was not only to serve others and support those wanting to hear the word, but also to be with God myself.

"Jesus told me that just because I am a woman gifted by God in hospitality and feel compelled to look after my guests, these things do not define me. I am capable of—I *am*—so much more."

Martha paused. The crowd was still entirely focused on her.

"Today, I was in the same position I was in that afternoon. However, Jesus did not want me to be the listener this time. He wanted me to be the speaker, to help you all learn about Jesus' life and the nature of God.

"My role here in Antioch was to be one of service. I was to manage logistics for gatherings. But as I found myself lamenting to God about Barnabas' absence, I recalled the encounter I had with Jesus that day in Bethany and stopped to pray for guidance. Then, with the help of Calliope here, who delivered a timely note from my sister, I realized what I was supposed to do. Jesus wanted me to speak to you about my encounters and relationship with him.

"I put all other aspects of this evening in God's hands. I did not have the time to organize food, refreshments, or even

---

7 Adapted from Luke 10:41-42 NIV

places where you could sit comfortably. I apologize for that, but what's most important is that you hear about Jesus."

There was silence for a few moments after Martha finished speaking. Martha could see the astonishment written all over their faces. This was clearly not what they expected to hear tonight.

For a moment, Martha began to worry about the silence. She felt an urgency to do something to break it. She found herself wishing once again that Barnabas was there to offer his dynamic speaking skills.

But then a gentle breeze blew through the courtyard and over the crowd's heads. It tapped Martha's brow, and she knew by the sense of peace that she felt at its touch that it was in fact the Holy Spirit. It danced around the room as the evening light sparkled through the courtyard. Martha could tell from the relaxed looks on the guests' faces that they, too, felt the Holy Spirit's presence. Their eyes delighted in the moment's splendor as they meditated upon Martha's message. The peaceful silence lasted several minutes.

A man broke the silence by rising to his feet and clearing his throat. He looked about thirty years old, tall, with classic Grecian facial features. His finely tailored clothes betrayed his privilege. He stood with his legs planted firmly shoulder-width apart and his head held high.

"I feel compelled to speak," he said purposefully, in Greek. "My name is Anastasios. This day could have been a very different one for me. It was supposed to be my wedding day. But the bride-to-be's family called off the wedding this morning because they found out that I wished to learn more about the message of Jesus. So, my friends, the wedding feast is prepared, but there is no one to enjoy it. That is, unless you would all like to join me.

"I feel like God is repurposing what was to be my wedding—making it something new—not a wedding but a banquet of friendship and new beginnings—an unexpected celebration—just like Martha's unexpected testimony.

"I am interested in learning how God wants to challenge me to be more than what I may have limited myself to be, just as Martha was challenged by Jesus. I am hungry to learn more about this God who is always bringing new life to situations that seem hopeless."

Many friendships were born that night. The wedding that did not happen became something more significant: a celebration of the church's birth at Antioch.

Photini's Daughter, Sofi,
Learns of Her Mother's Fate

Based on John 4:5–30

Sofi focused on counting as she breathed—one, two, three, four—hold—one, two, three, four, five, six—out. Doing this sometimes helped to calm her when her heart was thumping and her blood racing as they were now. She tried to focus her eyes on the centerpiece of the courtyard: a round sandstone pool, about ten steps in length, with a continuously flowing, three-tier ivory water fountain at its center. She wished the water feature could calm her anxiety, as it had on past occasions when she felt distressed. But today was different. Today, she was awaiting a message that would confirm her mother's fate.

A few months earlier, Sofi had awoken drenched in sweat and gasping for air. Images of the horrors the emperor had inflicted on her mother and family had suddenly intruded on her dreams. A message followed a few weeks later that confirmed the executions of both her brothers and some of her aunts. Her mother was still alive but remained captive.

Since that message, Sofi had hardly slept. She worried that if she fell asleep she would witness more horrors in her dreams, which would later be confirmed as realities. She lay in bed at night, beside her husband of twenty years, praying for her mother and pleading with God for her release.

As Sofi sat watching the water feature, she became aware that her fists were clenched. She recalled how, as a child, she constantly gripped various parts of her body. She shuddered as she remembered the yelling, shouting, and breaking of things, well after her bedtime, when she should have been asleep. Volatility had been the norm for most of her childhood, until one day a divine encounter changed her mother's and her family's life forever.

30 Years Earlier

I paced the small room, cradling my two younger brothers as they wailed. I bit my lip as I glanced outside to see if my mother was on her way back to the house. Sometimes, if I saw her coming, I could judge her mood by her gait and brace myself accordingly.

My mother walked purposely into our home and proceeded to pack our belongings into travel bags.

"Come, Sofi. We are leaving. I should have done this long ago, but I did not believe I was worthy."

I was glad to leave. I did not like living with a man who treated my mother like a slave—but I was also nervous about the unknown.

When we arrived at my mother's childhood home, two of my mother's sisters opened the door. Their reception was frosty, but my mother's parents, who were very frail, did not resist my mother's return.

Both of my mother's parents died not long after we came to stay.

The coldness of my mother's remaining family persisted. Every time they were unwelcoming, my mother responded with love and kindness. She was determined to reconcile with them, and eventually they thawed due to her infectious enthusiasm about the rabbi Jesus.

For the first time in my life, I could easily fall asleep. But my mother did not want to be idle. She wanted to follow Jesus more closely. She continued to work hard in her home of origin and prayed for a way forward.

My mother had always loved tapestry and creating unique designs. She had made several over time. One of them depicted her meeting with Jesus. While praying one day, she told me she saw an image of her waving her artwork in the air. Glittering light shone behind it, and with this vision, she felt inspired to take her works to the marketplace to sell.

The marketplace became a place not only where my mother spoke about Jesus but also where she tried to find out as much as she could about his movements.

One day a tall, graceful woman, immaculately dressed, approached her with several attendants. My mother's body stiffened. She was not used to seeing such fine people browse her wares. The lady went directly towards my mother's drapery portraying Jesus.

"I know this man," said the woman, whose name we soon learned was Joanna.

"Jesus?" my mother responded, astonished.

"The Messiah," Joanna returned.

My mother and Joanna locked eyes knowingly.

My mother burst out, "I met him once, and I want to follow him more closely. That is why I am here—to get money to go and follow him."

Joanna replied with equal intensity, "I have a story similar to yours, but this is not the time to tell it. I do not travel directly with Jesus, but I do stay close by. I organize various events and people to fund Jesus' ministry. You have an exquisite talent we could use for this purpose. Would you be interested in coming to live and work with us?"

My mother's eyes widened. "Where is he? I would like to see him again."

When Jesus first came to visit us, I could feel his presence in our home before I saw him. He spoke with such power and authority, yet his demeanor was not imposing. His gentle smile made me want to dance.

After Jesus had greeted the adults, he came over to me and introduced himself.

"Hi, Sofi," he said, with dancing eyes.

When I looked back at him, my soul enlarged with pride for who I was, reflected in his eyes. I blushed and giggled involuntarily. It was several days before I could stop smiling.

Before that moment, I had always felt invisible, even to myself. For as long as I could remember, I had always been preoccupied with meeting the needs of others—my mother, my siblings, and the relatives we lived with. Though I had felt safe when we first moved to my mother's family home, it was only when I met Jesus that I finally felt seen and cared for and had a clear sense of self.

Jesus ended up staying two days. When it was time for him to leave, I ran to him and hugged him more tightly than I had ever hugged anyone before. I was hopeful we would meet him again soon as my mother decided to take up Joanna's offer to live, work, and travel with her. My two unmarried aunts were also to come. I was sad to leave the home of my mother's family but excited about this new adventure.

With Joanna's connections, my mother was very successful. She made a substantial amount of money for Jesus' ministry. Joanna organized, where possible, a tutor for my siblings and me. But mostly, I worked with my mother, as did my two aunts. I was blessed to see Jesus again on several occasions.

After Jesus' death, resurrection, and ascension, my mother, brother, and I remained with Joanna and her group, and several years afterwards we moved to Antioch with them.

It was there that Anastasios and I met. He was fascinated by the stories I told about Jesus. Gradually, our friendship blossomed into something more. Anastasios told me he felt called to marry me and to create a loving home environment for one another, so that we might be an example of Jesus' love through our marriage, and perhaps, if we were so blessed, bring new life through our children.

Not long after we married, Agapi, our first child, was born. It was around this same time that my mother told me that Peter, Jesus' chosen successor, had asked her to travel away from Antioch to spread the good news.

On the day my mother left with her sisters and my younger brothers, my heart broke. It was now time to forge ahead and learn to be the rock for my family that my mother had been for me.

A messenger entered the courtyard and handed Sofi a small papyrus scroll. Sofi's trance broke. She inhaled and braced herself to open the note, which she was sure would confirm her mother's passing.

She unrolled the parchment, and the handwriting revealed that her mother was not its author. Sofi's heart sank, but she pressed on to read the text. She needed to have it confirmed that her mother had passed so she could permit herself to grieve properly.

Dear Sofi,

My name is Martinus Junius. I am a scribe in Nero's court, and your mother asked that I write to inform you of her passing after her death.

I am very sorry to tell you that your mother is no longer alive, although I am sure she now lives in heaven with Jesus.

I want to reassure you that although she was badly treated by Nero, her actual death was peaceful.

I also want to tell you that your mother most certainly did not die in vain. Her time in Rome bore fruit. Before your mother, aunts, and brothers died, they converted many in Nero's court, including me. The light of Christ shone through your mother's, aunts', and brothers' hearts in a way that was impossible to ignore. Those who converted to Christianity in Nero's court will ensure the message of Christ is carried further. We honor your family and want you to know how grateful we are for the gift of their lives and testimony.

Yours in Christ,

Martinus

Sofi looked up at the fountain in front of her. Her chest tightened. She put her hand on her belly, where a small bump was growing, and felt a small flutter. The new life within her steadied her and the fountain beckoned her forward.

She placed her hand in the fountain, lifted some water with it, and then watched it drip through her fingers. She remembered the words her mother had used when speaking to her about her first encounter with Jesus.

"Living water," Sofi said aloud.

She turned around and sat on the stone frame of the fountain.

"Jesus said, '. . .whoever drinks the water I give them will never thirst. Indeed, the water I give them will become in them a spring of water welling up to eternal life.'"[1]

----

1 John 4:14 NIV

Sofi closed her eyes and, for a moment, imagined she was at the well where her mother first met Jesus and that both were present with her.

The tightening in her chest softened.

"Jesus," Sofi prayed, "thank you for the gift of my mother and your presence in both of our lives. Please help me to carry on with my life here on earth so that I may continue to live as dedicated to you as my mother was."

Sofi kept her eyes closed. Her heart softened and expanded. Her cheeks flushed. She could see them in her mind: figures of water resembling her mother and Jesus rose out of the fountain and sat on either side of her. They each placed a hand on one of Sofi's. Her breathing became deeper and slower. She drank in their presence for as long as possible, until Jesus and her mother nodded to her and disappeared. Sofi opened her eyes.

Living water. Jesus had kept his promise to her mother—that if she followed him, he would give her the living water—the spring of water welling up to eternal life. Sofi looked up and raised her hands in a gesture of surrender.

"Jesus, I dedicate the rest of my story on this earth to you. I, too, like my mother before me, wish to drink your living water," she prayed.

Reflection on My Writing Pilgrimage—My Story of Jesus

Recently, I visited with a friend, and we talked about this book and the process I have gone through in writing it. My friend asked me how long I had been writing it, and I told her it had been at least twelve years. But when I think about it, this book is more than twelve years in the making. Any learning I have had in life, any experience of love, and any hardship I have worked through have all been a part of the process because it has all contributed to my understanding of myself, humanity, and Jesus.

My friend noted that I, as an individual, must have changed a lot over the past twelve years while I have been writing. This is true. I have entered several new seasons during this time and I have grown and matured through them. I started writing this book when I was single and about thirty years old, and I am now completing it at forty-two, as a married woman with three young children.

Through the stories in this book, Jesus accompanied me on my journey. He helped me heal and then led me through the next stages of my life. He introduced me to and made me feel comfortable with my husband and prepared me for marriage and family life. He also has helped me look forward to my life as an older woman and my mission going forward.

In writing this work, I sometimes found that images and ideas flowed freely, but at other times, even though I had spare moments to write, inspiration would not come. Later, I realized things that happened during this liminal space became a great inspiration for my writing.

My life experiences have helped me perceive a more multi-dimensional Jesus in my mind and heart as I can relate more fully to the lives and experiences of the Gospel women. The gift of picturing Jesus in my mind has allowed me to sense God as more intimate and personal and enabled me to center myself in times of turmoil. Through my imaginative journey, I better understand how God and Jesus interact with me during various seasons of my female life. The clarity of Jesus has also helped me to become more peaceful and content with him and myself.

Humanity needs Jesus. I hope this book provides others with a clearer glimpse of who he was and is, as writing it has done for me.

Suggested Format for Group Sharing

Feel free to use whatever format you would like to for a book club reflection or group sharing. The suggested format below is one that has worked for me in various reflection groups. It is more formal than other types of sharing groups, as it does not allow for open discussion during the meeting itself. (Of course, this can happen outside of the formal meeting.) I have found this allows for sharing and reflection to go deeper and also ensures each person in the group has an equal opportunity to contribute.

1. **Check In**

During a period of silence (3-4 minutes), members are invited to become still and aware of what is happening within them. Then, each group member shares this briefly in an image, phrase, or word or two. The group leader could use some gentle music if it helps to calm or center members.

The check-in is an integral part of the meeting, because:

a. By becoming aware at this time, people are sensitized to notice inner movements and shifts that occur during the meeting.

b. God loves, accepts, and calls us as we are—not as we think we should/could be. We come as we are to our God.

The exercise of noticing and naming what is happening inside us 'grounds' that gift of loving presence and acceptance, and members become more honest in expression and open in acceptance of one another's place. Being able to express hard/deep movements, feelings, thoughts, and desires and have them accepted is a gift of trust.

c. What comes up and is expressed here can surprise the speaker and provide fertile ground for inspiring and supporting one another in faith.

2. Readings

Read the relevant story in *Her Story of Jesus*. If you would like to, you can also read the Bible passage on which each story is based. A group member could read the passage and/or story aloud, or members could read it silently. Note that group members may have already read the relevant story from the book before attending the group. There may be a preference not to reread the story now. The reflections and questions I have written can also serve as promptings for sharing. You can discuss and decide as a group what is preferred here.

3. Sharing

Each person provides their reflection on how God spoke to them through the scripture passage or story and how this may reflect on something that is currently happening in their own life. The group can also use the discussion questions here as prompts. One person should speak at a time without being interrupted. Others in the group can ask questions to clarify a point that someone has shared.

However, this clarification should not lead to an open discussion among the group, nor should it be a personal reflection. Often sharing will go deeper when each person is given the opportunity to finish expressing their insights and be completely heard. Group members can reflect on how what someone has said in their sharing has resonated or affected them in the Second Round of Sharing—Exchange, outlined below.

There is no pressure to share. You can choose to pass on sharing if you do not feel comfortable doing so. You can also share as little or as much as you like.

4. Second Round of Sharing—Exchange

After each person has had the opportunity to share, group members can have another chance to reflect on what others in the group have said and how this has affected their thoughts and may have changed their own perspectives.

5. Check Out

Each group member can share a word or phrase to explain how their spirit may have been shifted during the meeting and how they are feeling after the meeting.

6. Final Prayer

Simple and brief. You can decide what sort of prayer or sending ritual you want to use here as a group. An example of one could be "Our Father."

The Our Father

Our Father,
who art in heaven,
hallowed be thy name;
thy kingdom come;
thy will be done on earth as it is in heaven.
Give us this day our daily bread;
and forgive us our trespasses
as we forgive those who trespass against us;
and lead us not into temptation,
but deliver us from evil.
Amen

Reflection on Expectations for Discussion Group

Before embarking on reading and discussing the stories in this book, it might be a good idea to meet with those in your group to discuss your expectations. You may also like to reflect together on your assumptions, interests, and understanding about the women characters of the Gospels. This will allow you to get to know one another a bit and help you confirm your points of view before beginning your journey. This early meeting may also allow you to gain deeper insights later on your journey with your group, not only in your own reflections, but also in your considerations of others' sharing. Below are some suggested questions for this initial meeting.

Introduction Questions

1. What are you hoping to gain out of this discussion group?

2. What first comes to mind when you think about women in the Bible?

3. Is there a female character you are particularly interested in or with whom you resonate? If so, why are you drawn to them?

4. Is there anything that strikes or baffles you about Jesus' relationship with women in the Gospels?

Reflection—Mary is Overshadowed by the Holy Spirit and Visits Elizabeth

Mary's story about how she conceived, broke the news to Joseph, and visited Elizabeth is fascinating. The Gospel account raises many questions for me that are left unanswered in the text.

The Bible is silent about what happened when the Holy Spirit overshadowed Mary, how Mary and Joseph reconciled, or when this happened in relation to the visitation.

I loved imagining the experience Mary may have had at the conception as it allowed me to enter into the mystery of this experience. I was reminded that as humans, even though we may have some spiritual experiences, we find it easy to doubt their veracity or even forget them soon after they take place. Mary may have experienced something unique at the annunciation and conception. However, she still had to face the reality of being pregnant but not to her betrothed, having to tell him about her pregnancy, facing the possibility of social ruin, and going through pregnancy, birth, and parenting by herself. The reality of her situation may have led her to doubt some of her mystical experiences. These reflections on Mary made me appreciate more how courageous she was as a woman. She followed God and what she believed his plan was for her despite the difficulties she faced.

In my story, God is more subtle in assisting Mary after the annunciation. God allowed Elizabeth to comfort and help her while Mary could also assist Elizabeth. I loved reflecting on how Mary and Elizabeth's lives may have proceeded during this time. It would have been a special time for two women supporting each other. It reminded me how God works through people to help us in difficult times. God was also working on Joseph during this time—to transform and prepare his heart for his role as Jesus' father.

Overall, reflecting on the annunciation, conception, and visitation story helped me experience aspects of this story I had not fully appreciated before—how strange this story was, how wondrous it was for Mary, but also how scary it was. I also enjoyed imagining the reconciliation of Joseph and Mary as it shows their relationship was real—not perfect—but they worked together to resolve issues, reconcile, and work together at what God wanted them to do.

I hope you can experience the annunciation, conception, and visitation in an inspiring way by reading this story.

Reflection Questions

1. Have you had any supernatural experiences of the Holy Spirit? If so, how did this experience shape your faith over time?

2. Have you ever been held by a close friend in a difficult time or season? What was this like? How can you express gratitude to your friend for helping you at this time and to God for holding you through this friend?

3. As you read the short story and reflect on the Gospel story of the annunciation, conception, and visitation, what other stirrings do you feel in your heart?

Reflection—Mary's Midwife Experiences the Birth of Jesus

After I gave birth to my first child, the nativity story changed for me forever. Giving birth is the most wonderful experience I have had in my life. It is also the rawest human experience I have had. I thought more about how the Christian tradition portrays the birth of Jesus. The Christmas Carol "Silent Night" illustrates the solemnity of Christ's birth. However, I do not think Jesus' birth would have been very silent, especially since animals surrounded Jesus in a stable. I feel the focus of this song does not give enough attention to the incredible human reality of birth. The birth of Jesus was the most crucial event in human history from a spiritual viewpoint, and I feel God would have specially marked it in a divine way.

I explored the more human aspect of Jesus' birth in this story.

There is no mention of a midwife being present at the birth of Jesus. Perhaps Joseph was the only one other than Mary at Jesus' birth, but he would have likely sought help to ensure Mary had proper care.

I was fortunate with my births to have good, competent midwives who supported me. Others have described their less positive experiences to me. In other contexts, I have also experienced older women who, for whatever reason, did not wish me to succeed in life and seemed to be against me. As they age, some women seem to mellow and become profound spiritual beings who are in tune and interested in others. However, another cohort of women seems lost and do not continue to advance in becoming lovelier versions of themselves. Instead, they become stagnant or even regress and can even become bitter. I imagined the midwife who attended to Mary to have been a mix of these two cohorts. She was somewhat angry, but her bitterness was rooted in her good intentions and love for others.

As I wrote this piece, although I set out to explore the human aspect of the story, I was struck unexpectedly by Jesus' divinity as a baby and the opening to Heaven that his birth caused. These transcendental elements of the nativity are what melted the midwife's heart.

Jesus was divine his whole life, and I am sure his holiness emanated from him even when he was a baby. A midwife who had attended many births would have noticed something different about him. Although babies often do have the power to melt hearts, this midwife's heart was hardened and required something more than a normal baby or a normal birth to be freed.

I enjoyed imagining and marveling at the nativity scene. I hope I have captured both the humanness and divinity of Jesus' birth and allowed you, as a reader, to experience more of both of these aspects of the nativity. Perhaps by entering into the story of the nativity in this way, something in your heart may melt, too.

Reflection Questions

1. How do you imagine you would have felt visiting Jesus as a newborn in the manger with Mary and Joseph present? What would it have been like to hold Jesus as a newborn?

2. Has your imagining of what the nativity would have been like changed over time? If you have physically given birth or attended a birth, has this changed your perspective on the nativity? If you have not been present at a birth, have you given birth to something spiritually that has changed your perspective on the nativity?

3. Is there anything else that stirs your heart after reading the short story and/or reflecting on the Gospel story of the nativity?

Reflection—Sepphora's Choice: The Bride at the Wedding at Cana Recalls Her Betrothal

My favorite Gospel story is The Wedding at Cana. There was so much to explore in this story of Jesus' first miracle that what started as one piece became two.

Sepphora's story explores how Jesus is connected to the wedding—how he is related to the bride and how he influences her decision to marry. Until I went through my discernment process about whether to get married, I did not understand the complexity and emotion of making this life-changing decision. I hope to convey some of that in this piece.

I experienced a lot of emotions that I did not expect when I met my husband. I had always thought that when I met the person I was supposed to be with, I would just know that I was meant to be with him and would not have any doubt. In my experience, there was an underlying peace about the situation. But I also experienced a lot of anxieties, and this was at least, in part, brought on by the realization that there would be losses for me in entering into marriage. I unexpectedly experienced anticipatory grief for the loss of my single life, although I knew I wanted to marry. Luckily, I found people and resources to talk this through and process, as Sepphora did in this story.

In my introduction, I touched on how, over the time I wrote this book, my picture of Jesus became clearer. I also touched on the fact that I had some negative experiences with men in my early adulthood. My negative experiences skewed how I experienced dating or attempted dating for a long time. I met my husband pretty soon after I was fully healed through a multi-faceted approach to healing-seeking. In my prayer, I had a clear experience of Jesus when contemplating my genuine fears about meeting someone. In my mind, Jesus clearly said to me, "Don't worry, he's friends with me."

There is a scene in Sepphora's story where she witnesses Jesus joking with her future husband, which allays many of her fears about getting married. This scene is inspired by my prayer experience.

I hope this story captures some of the complexities of the discernment process surrounding marriage (or another big decision) and how our spiritual lives and relationships, including our relationship with Jesus, can help us through that process.

Reflection Questions

1. Have you experienced a transition in your life that caused feelings you did not expect? How did you work through these feelings?

2. Have you ever had to make a decision in your life and experienced Jesus helping you to make it? What was this like?

3. Is there anything else that stirs your heart after reading the short story and/or reflecting on the Gospel story of the Wedding at Cana?

Reflection—Mara Serves at
the Wedding at Cana

How did there come to be a wine shortage in the first place? What were the preparations like for the wedding, and what type of people were the servants in the house hosting the wedding? How did Mary find out about the issue with the wine from these servants, and how did these servants resolve this problem? I was interested in the details that led to Jesus' first miracle—wine, water, feasting and food, a wedding, and his relationship with his mother.

Exploring these details first helped me understand more about Jesus' relationships and interactions with the other characters in this story. It then enabled me to see the miracle Jesus performed more clearly and how it affected those at the wedding. Perhaps more importantly, this imaginative experience cemented for me the solid relationship Jesus had with his mother. He showed this in how he listened to and respected her.

In writing this story, I came to wonder more about how Jesus interacted with those around him in truly earthly ways. These human interactions often become luminous in unexpected and mysterious ways, as they did in the story about the wedding at Cana. Some other examples in the Gospels of where this happens are Jesus feeding the five thousand, and eats fish after his resurrection.

By reading this story, I hope you can also find wonder in the mystery of how Jesus and God interact with us in such tangible and sensual yet divine and profound ways.

Reflection Questions

1. Have you ever had something go wrong in a particularly stressful situation and found the problem to be resolved in such an unexpected way that you were sure it had God's hand on it? What was it like to experience this?

2. Have you had an experience of Jesus making wine out of water in your own life? If so, what was it, and how did you recognize that God was responsible for the transformation?

3. Does this story offer you a new perspective on the relationship between Jesus and his mother?

Reflection—Anya, the Bleeding Woman, is Healed

This piece was one of the easiest to write, and I am still trying to figure out why. I could resonate with Anya despite the age gap because I have experienced some of the frustration of ongoing health issues related to being female that did not have an easy fix. However, what I experienced was very minor compared to what Anya experienced.

I was interested in how she lived despite her poverty and illness. Her quality of life must have been low, and perhaps she was supported by one or two friends or family members. She must have been exhausted from her efforts to find healing and near to giving up. But something about Jesus made her try one more time—and her efforts paid off.

Anya must have heard something about Jesus that stirred her to make a determined effort to seek healing from him. She had been to see so many physicians. She spent her savings seeking a cure for something that not only was very personal and embarrassing but also precluded her from participating in Jewish religious activities such as going to the temple.

I was interested to know how Anya may have received news about Jesus and how she believed he could heal her. Exploring this helped me understand more about Jesus' magnetism. This magnetism must have had something unique—a sense of approachability. Despite him being such a solid, charismatic figure, characters like Anya, despite fears they may have held, were determined to seek him out.

Anya recognized this magnetism as love, and it was this love that Jesus was using to heal.

I hope you can experience this magnetic love of Jesus when reading this piece.

Reflection Questions

1. Have you experienced healing (either physical, psychological, or spiritual) from an ailment or trauma in your own life that has drawn you closer to God or given you a deeper understanding of yourself or life?

2. What do you think distinguished Jesus from other healers at the time that led Anya to seek healing from him despite her not having success with other healers/physicians?

3. Did reading the short story and/or reflecting on the Gospel story of the "Bleeding Woman" stir anything else in your heart?

Reflection—*Talitha Koumi*— Jesus Heals a Little Girl

I have always been curious about near-death experiences. Many people (including a childhood neighbor of mine) recall experiences of being parted from their bodies, experiencing mystical feelings, and sometimes meeting people who have passed away before returning.[1] Saint Paul, the Apostle, had one of these experiences, although he only mentions it once in his writings.[2] I imagined the little girl that Jesus healed would have had some kind of experience like this, and I wanted to imagine what her healing was like from her perspective and how it affected her and her family.

I began writing this piece by thinking about what I did as a twelve-year-old and where my headspace was. I reflected that many things I did would have been very different from what a girl in Jesus' era would have done. Many of the worries and anxieties of the modern day would not translate. However, there are still things my twelve-year-old self and this healed girl would share. Like me, she too would have been reliant on her parents, and she also could have been curious and possibly anxious about her future life.

By connecting again with my twelve-year-old self, I was able to experience Jesus from a place of innocence and simplicity in the event of being brought back to life. I also

1 Michael Zigarelli, "Near-Death Experiences and the Emerging Implications for Christian Theology", *Christian Scholar's Review*, 53:2, 75-97, accessed June 1, 2025, https://christianscholars. com/near-death-experiences-and-the-emerging-implications-for-christian-theology/
2 2 Corinthians 12:1–5

enjoyed imagining what the encounter of the little girl's parents would have been like and the journey of emotion they went on in caring for her, seeking out Jesus for healing, and then having her miraculously healed. At the end of the piece, I imagine the family together at Jesus' entrance into Jerusalem before his sentencing, execution, and resurrection. Imagining this gave me a clearer understanding of how Jesus influenced not only the lives of those he healed but also the lives of all those around him.

I hope that, in reading this piece, you will be amazed at the little girl's healing and how it ricocheted throughout her family and community.

Reflection Questions

1. Have you ever had a supernatural experience you could not explain or heard someone's testimony about something like this? Did it change your faith?

2. Was your image of or relationship with Jesus different when you were a child? If so, how? How has your image or relationship changed? Has this been a positive or negative thing? Can you think of any specific reasons for this change?

3. Is there something in your life that needs healing? Can you imagine being the girl in this story and being healed in this special way by Jesus? You may like to spend a few moments imagining this scene and seeing if your feelings or insights into your situation change. What was this experience like for you?

Reflection—A Transformative Meeting and a Last Act of Service

The story of Jesus in the temple does not go into detail about how Jesus managed by himself in the three days when he was unintentionally left behind by his family. The story of the last supper also does not provide details about who prepared Jesus' final meal. In this story, I have imagined the background to these two stories and have drawn them together.

I enjoyed imagining what Jesus was like as a child, how he was tender towards his peers, and how a relationship from his childhood translated into adulthood. With this imagining, I believe Jesus was helping me to understand there is no need to fear this older Jesus—he truly is approachable. I think sitting with the boy Jesus in this story and then journeying towards adulthood as the girl and then the woman in the story helped to heal some of my psychological trauma/wounds that were making it difficult to perceive the adult Jesus in my mind.

This story also made me grateful for other children in my childhood who behaved like Jesus in this story. I know some children comforted and included me when I felt excluded, and this had a significant impact on me at the time, which I am sure has also carried over into my adult life.

Overall, imagining this story made me experience Jesus' tenderness uniquely, making me feel much more comfortable with him. I hope you had a similar experience reading this story.

Reflection Questions

1. Was there a friend in your childhood who was Jesus for you and made a significant difference in your life?

2. Do you find it easier or harder to imagine the young Jesus rather than the adult Jesus? If the experience of imagining Jesus as a boy is different, can you explain why?

3. Do you have any psychological wounds from your childhood that remain unhealed? Do you think sitting with the childhood Jesus as your childhood self, letting Jesus comfort you, could help your healing? Why or why not?

Reflection—Pilate's Wife's Story

"What is truth?"

Pilate's question is just as relevant today as it was then, if not more so. The availability of information accessible 24/7 at our fingertips has made it more difficult to discern what is true, as various sources present multiple truths. I am a sensitive, analytical person who is prone to anxiety, which sometimes manifests in obsessions. I also am very interested in truth. These combined personality traits have meant that I have entered a state of turmoil several times after reading the news and trying to discern the truth.

Jesus does not offer a version of facts about an actual event. Instead, he offers himself: "I am the way, the truth, and the life." He does not provide this answer to Pilate in the story but to his disciples earlier on, before he is put on trial and sentenced. However, he does tell Pilate that he has come to "testify to the truth."

In these times of turmoil, returning to Jesus and praying with him in whatever way is best has helped me regain my peace. I also find it comforting to know that in Jesus' day, people grappled with the same question: "What is truth?" It gives me some reassurance that things are not going from better to worse but perhaps have always been about the same—despite what the news appears to portray.

This story was the first one I was inspired to write. I believe this is for a few reasons.

Firstly, this story shows the historical and political context in which Jesus lived and sets the scene for my pilgrimage.

Secondly, Claudia and Jesus do not interact directly. She experiences him from afar, and this is where I was most comfortable when I started out on this imaginative pilgrimage. Jesus is gentle and meets me where I am most comfortable.

Finally, Jesus wanted to show me upfront how relevant he is. Pilate articulates a question that is still very prominent today: What is truth?

Interestingly, Claudia was greatly affected by what was happening with Jesus. There could be several reasons for this. Perhaps she had followed Jesus' ministry and knew much about him and his message. Or maybe she intuited that something much more significant was going on than she could see.

I hope that you are comforted by how Jesus answers Pilate's questions about truth and that you experience Jesus' conversation with Pilate in a fresh way as you read this story.

Reflection Questions

1. What questions of truth do we grapple with today as a society?

2. Are there any questions about the truth that you grapple with individually?

3. Have you ever had a vivid dream that has impacted you so much that it has influenced your behavior like Pilate's wife's did? If so, how did it affect you, and did it impact the trajectory of your life?

4. Is there anything else that stirs your heart after reading the short story and reflecting on the Gospel story of Pilate's wife?

Reflection—Joanna Experiences the Resurrection of Jesus

This story explores the aftermath of Jesus' death for his female followers and considers its effect on Joanna in particular.

I wrote this piece over several years and got stuck several times along the way. The resurrection is perhaps the most challenging part of the Gospels for many of us to imagine because it is so strange.

In writing this story, I discovered many aspects of the resurrection story that I had not noticed before. I had never considered what happened after Jesus' body left the cross, who was present at his burial, what the walk home from the tomb was like, and the mood of the disciples after his execution. The man they had come to rely upon, who had given them hope that something more significant than any of them could imagine was happening, was dead. Many of these people had given up a great deal to follow him. I felt their anger, disbelief, denial, and shock by entering into the story.

I imagined that the women would have been very efficient. Despite what had happened, they organized themselves to make sure they could treat Jesus' body properly on the third day after his death. Perhaps this was calming for them, but it is still commendable what they managed to do.

Piecing together details of what the days after Jesus died were like for Joanna helped me prepare for how I experienced this event through her eyes. Then, when I arrived at the part of the story where Joanna was on the way to the tomb, knocked down by the "earthquake" but unable to see further, I became stuck for a long time.

I remained on the ground but found my hands were holding onto Jesus' feet. Still, I could not—or, perhaps, I was not ready—to look up. Many times I've laid in this place with my prayer—at Jesus' feet—when I struggled and felt there was no way forward. With weak faith, I chose to keep my hands on Jesus' feet and not look up.

I wondered why I could not or was not ready to look up. Sometimes, seeing the resurrected Jesus seemed too much for me. It could overwhelm me. But then I began to remind myself Jesus is gentle and he does not wish to overwhelm me.

I realized I was putting too much pressure on myself to capture the enormity of the resurrection in one glance, both in my imagination and in my written piece. Looking up at Jesus is just one glance. The story doesn't end there. There is a whole season of Easter. After all, the resurrection is probably something we can never fully understand in this life. It is something we continually find out more about in our faith journeys each day.

Overall, what I gained from entering this story was a greater appreciation of the wonder, strangeness, brilliance, and enormity of the resurrection. I hope that by reading my story, you gain some of that too.

Reflection Questions

1. Have you ever struggled with a belief in the resurrection? If so, what parts do you find challenging?

2. Are there any little resurrections in your life that you can identify? Would you like to share one or more of these resurrection stories?

3. Was there a part of this story that particularly touched or struck you? If so, why did it touch you? You may like to share about this.

Reflection—Martha's Ministry in Antioch

I love the characters of Mary and Martha of Bethany. Their different personalities highlight how different we can be as humans, and some of Jesus' interactions with the two sisters are surprising. I always admired Martha as an efficient soul with the courage to speak up when she believed something was wrong. Mary always seemed ethereal; she strikes me as being extremely sensitive and aware of how others felt.

In the story where Martha becomes upset because her sister is not helping her serve their guests, I naturally identified with Martha more than Mary and was alert to the injustice of Martha's situation until a wise woman explained her interpretation of this story. Jesus is telling Martha that she is more than just a servant in her role as a woman. She and Mary had just as much right as the men to sit and learn from him and did not need to limit themselves to the service of those learning from Jesus. Of course, knowing how to serve and entertain others comes with incredible talent and skill; I do not think Jesus wanted to dismiss this in Martha, but let her know there is more to who she is in him.

In this piece, I imagine what the lives of these women would have been like following Jesus' death and how they worked together, leaning on each other in their differences to support one another in their ministries.

I believe women have a special gift. They are the glue that holds society together in their everyday interactions of love with one another and their community. These interactions may go unnoticed in the public sphere, but collectively, they are more powerful manifestations of love than any great earthly achievement. I believe we should recognize and acknowledge this more as a society but also not limit women only to the home sphere. I hope I have captured this message in my story.

Reflection Questions

1. Who do you identify more with, Mary or Martha?

2. What do you think Jesus meant when he told Martha that Mary had chosen the better part?

3. What are the strengths that you identify yourself with most?

4. Are there parts of yourself that you may be limiting because you have dismissed them or feel not good enough/worthy enough to explore?

Reflection—Photini's Daughter, Sofi, Learns of Her Mother's Fate

The story of the Samaritan woman who meets Jesus at the well is fascinating. It raises many questions about her character history, which I have explored in this piece. When I researched the Samaritan woman, I found quite a bit written about what may have happened to her after she met with Jesus. Lore records her name as Photini, and she eventually died a martyr by the hand of Emperor Nero in Rome. I wanted to explore what happened after Jesus' death and resurrection to some of the women who encountered him in their lives, and I thought Photini's daughter's eyes might be a good vantage point from which to do this.[1]

Interestingly, it was not any special privilege or right that Jesus granted to women that changed their lives, but it was his ability to see them for what they were, love them, and reflect that love and knowledge of themselves. This love sets them free. Perhaps this is a little of the living water he describes in his conversation with Photini.

Similarly, how Jesus interacted with women and his behavior toward them changed men's attitudes towards women. Sofi, in this piece, ends up in a loving marriage despite having grown up as a child in a house characterized

---

[1] "St Photini, The Samaritan Woman - Patron Saint of OCL", *Orthodox Christian Laity*, adapted from *Saints and Sisterhood: The Lives of Forty-Eight Holy Women*, accessed May 30, 2025, https://ocl.org/orthodox-christian-laity/st-photini-patron-saint-of-ocl/

by domestic violence. Her husband, Anastasios, was drawn to Christianity and receptive to the stories he heard about Jesus interacting with women (as I detailed in the previous story about Martha's ministry).

I imagined that Sofi would have been so grateful to Jesus and her mother for turning her life around.

I love how Jesus describes himself as the giver of living water. This imagery is beautiful and powerful. I imagined the daughter of the Samaritan woman being comforted in her grief by a dazzling experience of Jesus and her mother being with her at the water feature, reminiscent of the well where her mother first encountered Jesus. I did not have this particular image after my father's death, but I felt consoled spiritually at times soon after his passing so that I could resonate with Sofi's experience. Her experience reassures her that this life is not the end.

I hope that by reading this story, you will experience the budding of early Christianity in the way some women of that era experienced it. May you find comfort and delight in Sofi's image of living water.

Reflection Questions

1. Has there been someone in your life that experienced a significant conversion? How did this affect those who were closely associated with them?

2. Has your family or a family you know experienced any intergenerational healing? Or, is there an intergenerational hurt that remains in your family? If so, can you ask Jesus to come into this space and heal it?

3. Have you had a comforting spiritual experience after the death of a loved one? What was it like, and how did it change you?

4. What are your thoughts or understanding about what Jesus describes as "living water"? Where is the living water in your own life?

Final Questions

1. Has your understanding of Jesus changed since reading this book or participating in this group?

2. Which character are you most drawn to now? Is this different from the character you were drawn to before starting this reading/discussion journey?

3. Which character do you aspire to become more like?

4. Are there any Gospel stories you would like to explore in more detail through imagination or biblical study?

Acknowledgments

Firstly, I would like to thank Samantha Cabrera, owner of Calla Press Publishing, for giving me the opportunity to publish *Her Story of Jesus* and for designing its magnificent book cover. Thank you, Samantha, for believing in this book and my writing. Thank you also to Madison Aichele, Executive Director of Calla Press Publishing, who has patiently read several drafts and given me constructive, encouraging feedback throughout the editing process. I would also like to thank all the wonderful editors at Calla Press Publishing.

Thank you to *Foreshadow Magazine*, *Macrina Magazine*, *Calla Press Literary Journal*, and the *Agape Review* for publishing some earlier versions of my stories. This encouraged me to complete this book's writing journey.

There are several books that inspired me to write *Her Story of Jesus*. I would like to thank Anita Diamant, author of *The Red Tent*, Vanessa L. Ochs, author of *Sarah Laughed*, and Paula Gooder, author of *Phoebe*, for their beautiful stories.

I was fortunate enough to come across some of the work of the historian and biblical scholars Joan Taylor and Helen Bond about the women who were close to Jesus. A two-part series featuring Taylor and Bond's research into Jesus' female disciples can be found on the Australian Broadcasting Corporation's program Compass. I found this historical perspective very helpful when I was drafting several of my short stories in *Her Story or Jesus*, and I would like to thank these historians for their work on this topic.

This book would not have been created without the Ignatian community in Australia, who have invested a lot into the formation of my spirituality. For this, I am most grateful.

Similarly, my inspiration would not have come without my having encountered all of the people in my life who have shown me the love of Jesus. I am incredibly blessed to have a loving husband, wonderful, faithful parents, and many other parental figures, friends, and family who have done so.

Finally and most of all, thank you to God for the gift of life and this experience of having your story flow through me in writing.

About the Author

Katie Sampias is a wife and mother of three young children. She lives in Brisbane, Australia, where she grew up in a busy household with four brothers and was the only girl. She fell in love with all aspects of stories as a child—reading, writing, imagining, investigating, and researching them. At the age of twelve, she won a trip to Vanuatu for submitting stories and poems to the local paper. Katie always dreamt of being a published author, and having *Her Story of Jesus* published is the realization of that dream.

Despite initially pursuing other studies at university in humanities and law, the desire to pursue writing never left her. In her late twenties she went back to study Journalism, and during those studies took courses on historical fiction and life writing. The first story written for *Her Story of Jesus* was written for assessment as a historical fiction piece during these studies.

In her spare time, apart from writing, you can find Katie exercising, getting a relaxing treatment or socializing with friends and family.

Katie has lived in Ireland, Australia, and the United States.

Connect with Katie here:

https://substack.com/@katiesampias
https://instagram.com/surfingwhitewaves
https://katiesampias.com
https://www.facebook.com/surfingwhitewaves/

www.ingramcontent.com/pod-product-compliance
Lightning Source LLC
Chambersburg PA
CBHW020809310726
48969CB00002B/779